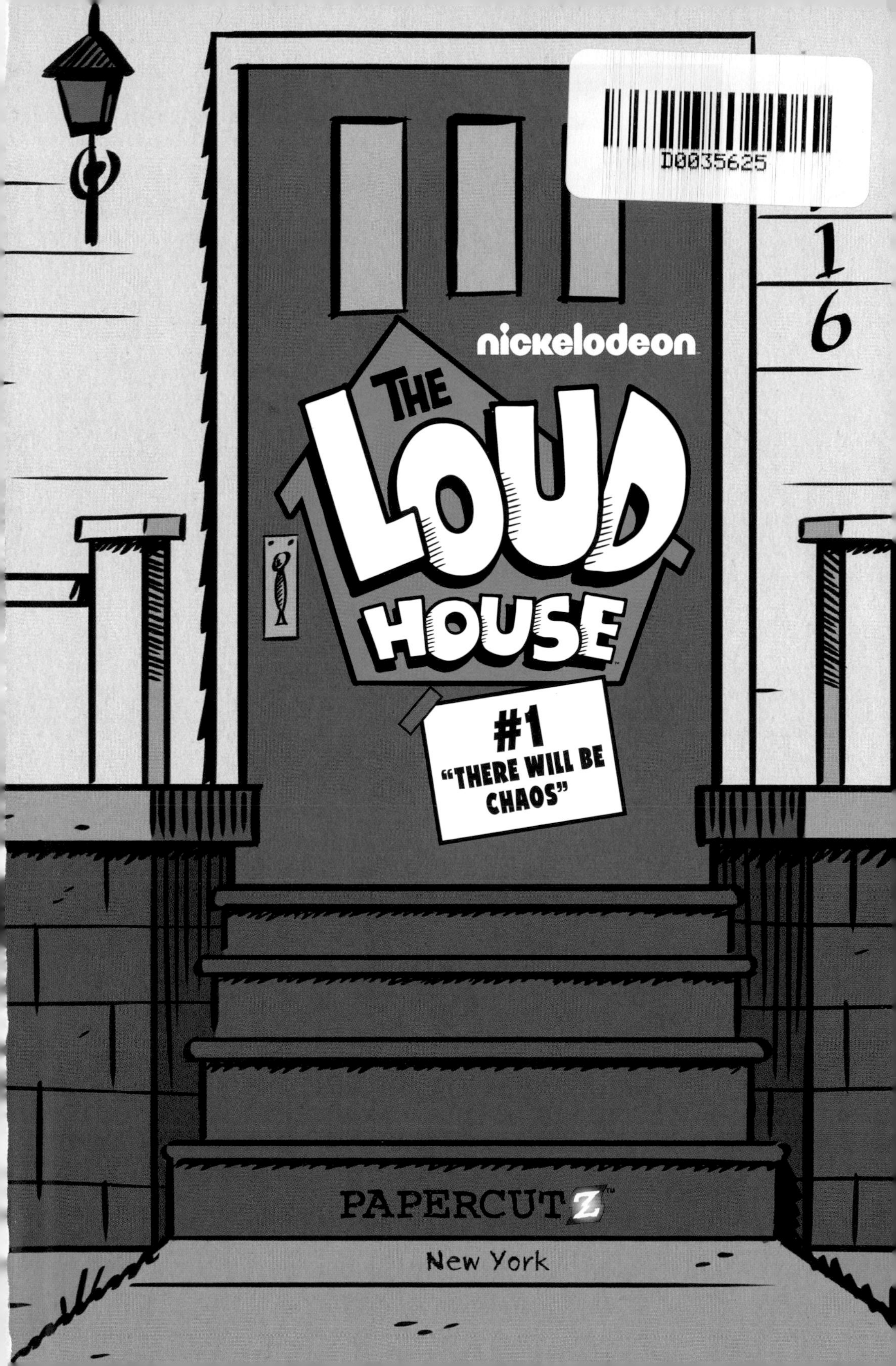
nickelodeon
THE LOUD HOUSE
#1
"THERE WILL BE CHAOS"
16
PAPERCUTZ
New York

nickelodeon GRAPHIC NOVELS AVAILABLE FROM PAPERCUTZ

nickelodeon
PANDEMONIUM!
CHANNELING FUN
PAPERCUTZ

NICKELODEON PANDEMONIUM
#1 "Channeling Fun"

nickelodeon
PANDEMONIUM!
SPIES AND DUCKTECTIVES
A TOP SECRET COLLECTION OF COMICS
TOP SECRET
PAPERCUTZ

NICKELODEON PANDEMONIUM
#2 "Spies and Ducktectives"

NICKELODEON'S HIT NEW ANIMATED SHOW
nickelodeon
THE LOUD HOUSE
THERE WILL BE CHAOS
PAPERCUTZ

LOUD HOUSE
#1 "There Will Be Chaos"

COMING SOON

nickelodeon
THE LOUD HOUSE
THERE WILL BE CHAOS
PAPERCUTZ

LOUD HOUSE
#2 "There Will Be More Chaos"

nickelodeon
SANJAY AND CRAIG
FIGHT THE FUTURE WITH FLAVOR!
PAPERCUTZ

SANJAY AND CRAIG
#1 "Fight the Future with Flavor"

nickelodeon
SANJAY AND CRAIG
NEW KID ON THE BLOCK
PAPERCUTZ

SANJAY AND CRAIG
#2 "New Kid on the Block"

nickelodeon
STORY TIME WITH
SANJAY AND CRAIG
PAPERCUTZ

SANJAY AND CRAIG
#3 "Story Time with Sanjay and Craig"

nickelodeon
PIG GOAT BANANA CRICKET
Orgle Borgle Selfie Simple-Dee-Doo!
PAPERCUTZ

PIG GOAT BANANA CRICKET
#1 "Orgle Borgle Selfie Simple-Dee Doo!"

nickelodeon
BREADWINNERS
JOURNEY TO THE BOTTOM OF THE SEATS
PAPERCUTZ

BREADWINNERS
#1 "Journey to the Bottom of the Seats"

nickelodeon
BREADWINNERS
Buhdeuce Rocks the Rocket
PAPERCUTZ

BREADWINNERS
#2 "Buhdeuce Rocks the Rocket"

nickelodeon
HARVEY BEAKS
INSIDE JOKE
PAPERCUTZ

HARVEY BEAKS
#1 "Inside Joke"

nickelodeon
THE FEEL-GOOD GRAPHIC NOVEL!
HARVEY BEAKS
IT'S CRAZY TIME!
PAPERCUTZ

HARVEY BEAKS
#2 "It's Crazy Time"

Nickelodeon graphic novels are available for $7.99 each in paperback, $12.99 each in hardcover. Available from booksellers everywhere. You can also order online from Papercutz.com, or call 1-800-886-1223, Monday through Friday, 9-5 EST. MC, Visa, and AmEx accepted. To order by mail, please add $4.00 for postage and handling for the first book ordered, $1.00 for each additional book and make check payable to NBM Publishing. Send to: Papercutz, 160 Broadway, Suite 700, East Wing, New York, NY 10038.

Nickelodeon Graphic Novels are also available digitally wherever e-books are sold.

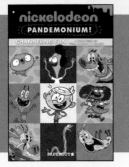

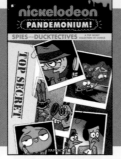

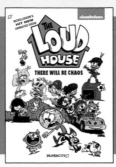

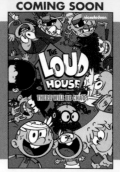

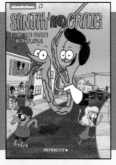

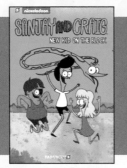

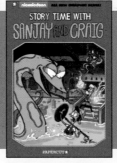

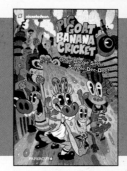

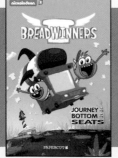

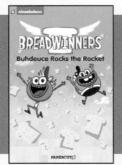

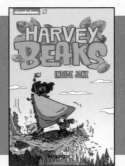

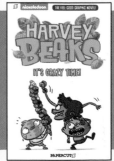

THE LOUD HOUSE

THERE WILL BE CHAOS

#1

Mom needs you to find the remote for Lincoln! Please go to page 7 to start looking!

Meet the Loud Family
5

Watch Out for Papercutz
58

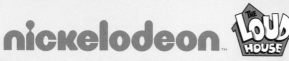

nickelodeon THE LOUD HOUSE #1 "THERE WILL BE CHAOS"

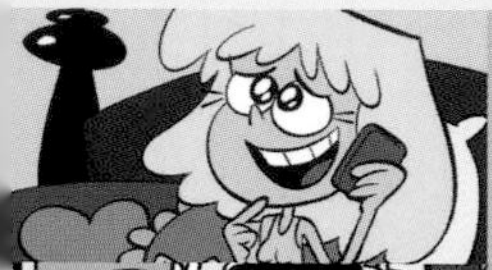

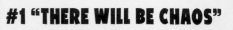

"NO, YOU HANG UP"
AMANDA RYNDA—
Writer, Artist, Letterer, Colorist

"THE SPOT"
DIEM DOAN—Writer, Artist, Letterer
AMANDA RYNDA—Colorist

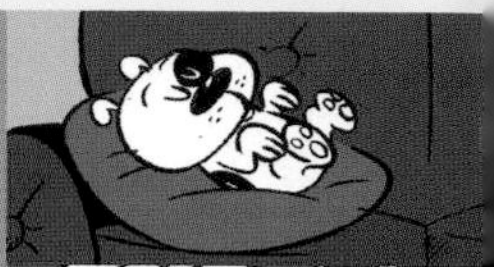

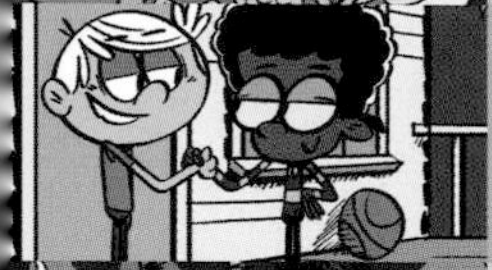

"THE HANDSHAKE"
SAMMIE CROWLEY & WHITNEY WETTA—Writers
KYLE MARSHALL—Artist, Letterer
AMANDA RYNDA—Colorist

"NO SPOILERS"
SAMMIE CROWLEY & WHITNEY WETTA—Writers
JORDAN KOCH—Artist, Letterer
ASHLEY KLIMENT—Colorist

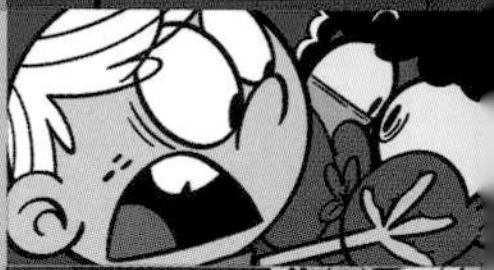

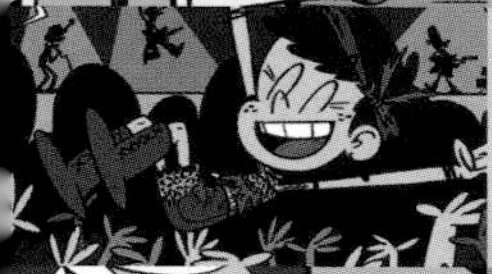

"LUNA'S NEW THREADS"
JORDAN ROSATO—Writer, Artist, Letterer
AMANDA RYNDA—Colorist

"THE CALL"
SAMMIE CROWLEY & WHITNEY WETTA—Writers
MIGUEL PUGA—Artist, Letterer
ASHLEY KLIMENT—Colorist

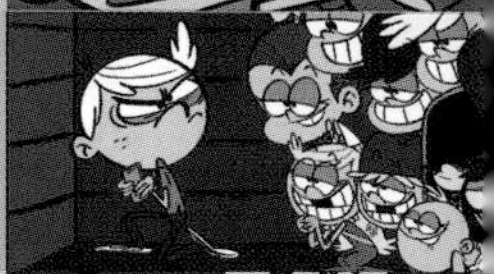

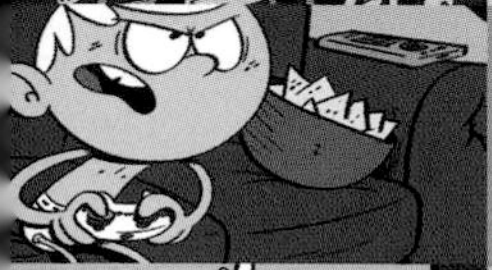

"VIDEO GAME MOJO"
JARED MORGAN—Writer, Artist, Letterer
HALLIE WILSON—Colorist

"VERY SUPERSTITIOUS"
TODD OMAN—Writer, Artist, Letterer
ASHLEY KLIMENT—Colorist

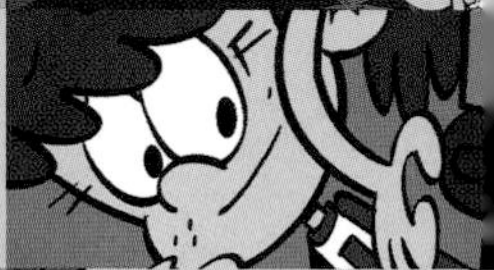

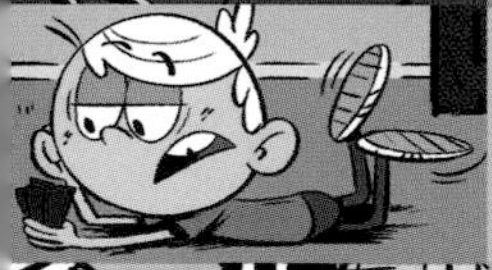

"GONE FISHING"
JARED MORGAN—Writer, Artist, Letterer
AMANDA RYNDA—Colorist

"HERE COMES THE AIRPLANE"
DAVID KING—
Writer, Artist, Letterer, Colorist

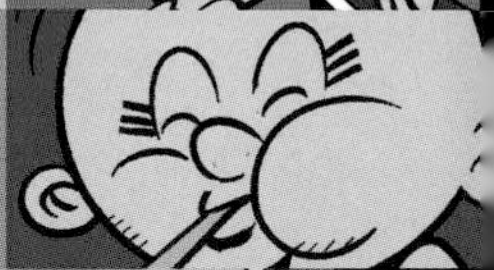

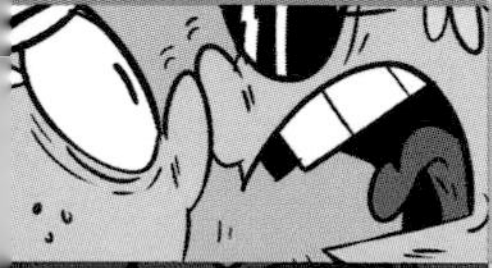

"LOUD AND ORDER"
KEVIN SULLIVAN—Writer
ARI CASTLETON—Artist, Letterer
AMANDA RYNDA—Colorist

"WALL WALKER"
JORDAN ROSATO—Writer, Artist, Letterer
AMANDA RYNDA—Colorist

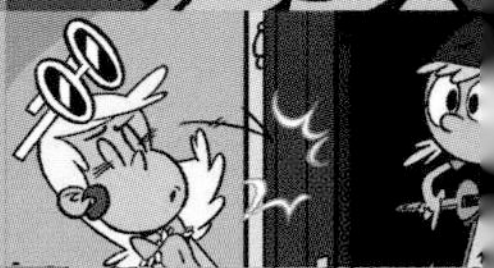

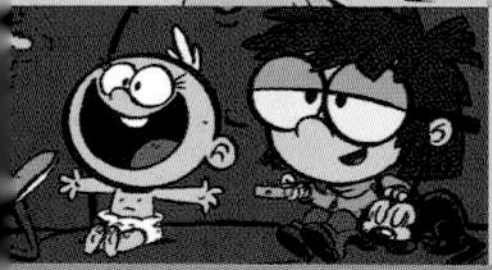

"SHOCKER"
MIGUEL PUGA—Writer, Artist, Letterer
AMANDA RYNDA—Colorist

"LOST CONTROL"
SAMMIE CROWLEY, WHITNEY WETTA & KARLA SAKAS SHROPSHIRE—Writers
JORDAN KOCH—Artist, Letterer
AMANDA RYNDA—Colorist

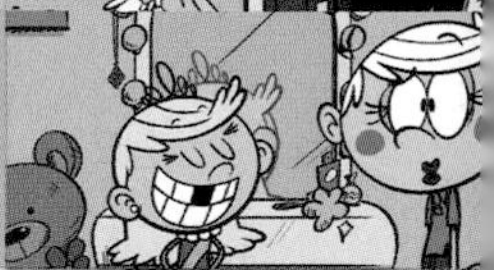

THE LOUD HOUSE
Created by CHRIS SAVINO

"TOUGHEST GUY IN HISTORY"
ERIC ESQUIVEL—Writer
DAVID DEGRAND—Artist
TOM ORZECHOWSKI—Letterer
LAURIE E. SMITH—Colorist
Pig Goat Banana Cricket created by
JOHNNY RYAN and DAVE COOPER

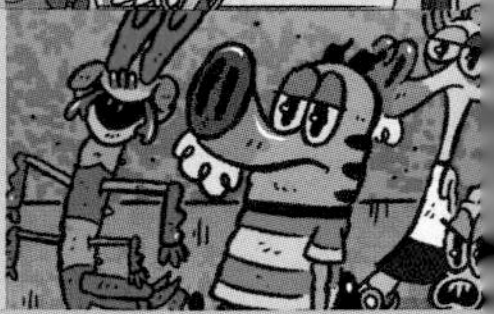

CHRIS SAVINO — Cover Artist
JORDAN ROSATO — Endpapers
JAMES SALERNO — Sr. Art Director/Nickelodeon
DAWN GUZZO — Design/Production
SASHA KIMIATEK — Production Coordinator
JEFF WHITMAN — Editor
JOAN HILTY — Comics Editor/Nickelodeon
JIM SALICRUP
Editor-in-Chief

ISBN: 978-1-62991-740-5 paperback edition
ISBN: 978-1-62991-741-2 hardcover edition

Printed in USA
August 2018

Distributed by Macmillan
Fifth Printing

MEET THE LOUD FAMILY

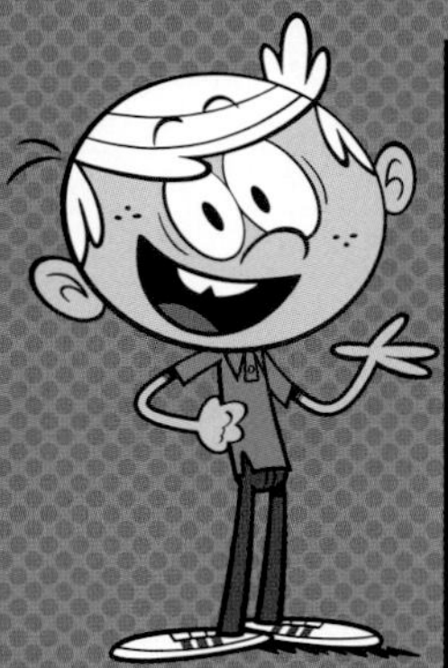

LINCOLN LOUD
THE MIDDLE CHILD (11)

At 11 years old, Lincoln is the middle child, with five older sisters and five younger sisters. He has learned that surviving the Loud household means staying a step ahead. He's the man with a plan, always coming up with a way to get what he wants or deal with a problem, even if things inevitably go wrong. Being the only boy comes with some perks. Lincoln gets his own room – even if it's just a converted linen closet. On the other hand, being the only boy also means he sometimes gets a little too much attention from his sisters. They mother him, tease him, and use him as the occasional lab rat or fashion show participant. Lincoln's sisters may drive him crazy, but he loves them and is always willing to help out if they need him.

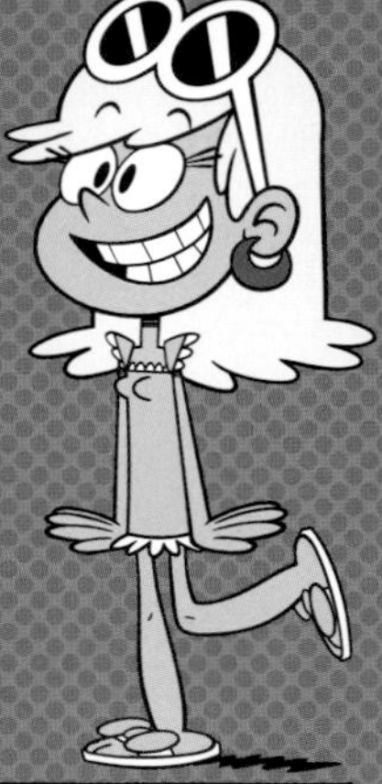

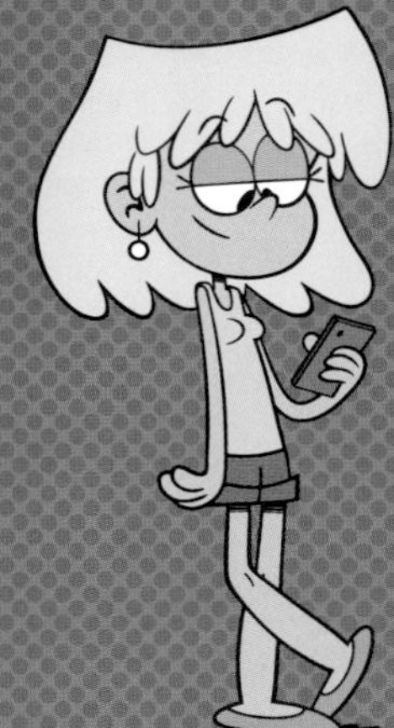

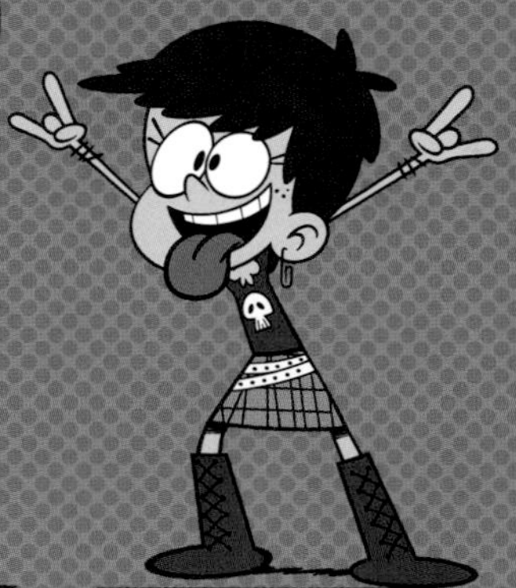

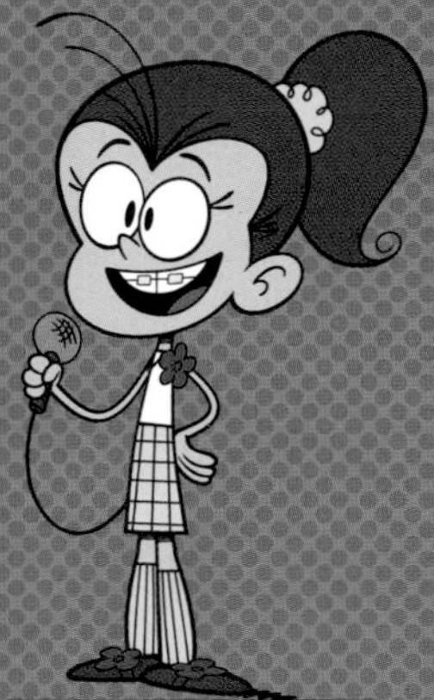

LENI LOUD
THE FASHIONISTA (16)

Leni is the ditsiest of the Loud sisters. She spends most of her time designing outfits and accessorizing (though she probably can't spell the word). She is easily distracted by shiny objects, always falls for Luan's pranks, and sometimes walks into walls when she's talking (she's not great at doing two things at once). Leni might be flighty, but she's the sweetest of the Loud siblings and truly has a heart of gold (even though she's pretty sure it's a heart of blood).

LORI LOUD
THE OLDEST (17)

As the first-born child of the Loud clan, Lori sees herself as the boss of all her siblings. She feels she's paved the way for them and deserves extra respect. Her signature traits are rolling her eyes, texting her boyfriend Bobby, and literally saying "literally" all the time. Because she's the oldest and most experienced sibling, Lori can be a great ally, so it pays to stay on her good side.

LUNA LOUD
THE ROCK STAR (15)

Luna is loud, boisterous and freewheeling, and her energy is always cranked to 11. She thinks about music so much that she even talks in song lyrics. On the off chance she doesn't have her guitar with her, everything can and will be turned into a musical instrument. You can always count on Luna to help out, and she'll do most anything you ask, as long as you're okay with her supplying a rocking guitar accompaniment.

LUAN LOUD
THE JOKESTER (14)

Luan's a standup comedienne who provides a nonstop barrage of silly puns. She's big on prop comedy too – squirting flowers and whoopee cushions – so you have to be on your toes whenever she's around. She loves to pull pranks and is a really good ventriloquist – she is often found doing bits with her dummy, Mr. Coconuts. Luan never lets anything get her down; to her, laughter IS the best medicine.

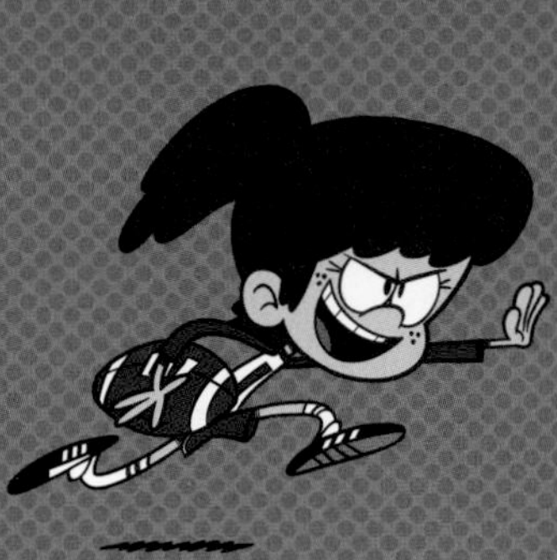

LYNN LOUD
THE ATHLETE (13)

Lynn is athletic and full of energy and is always looking for a teammate. With her, it's all sports all the time. She'll turn anything into a sport. Putting away eggs? Jump shot! Score! Cleaning up the eggs? Slap shot! Score! Lynn is very competitive, tends to be superstitious about her teams, and accepts almost any dare.

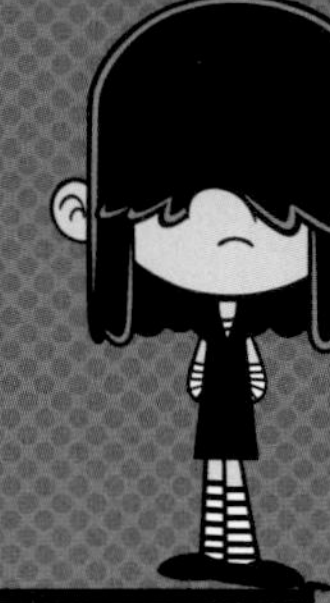

LUCY LOUD
THE EMO (8)

You can always count on Lucy to give the morbid point of view in any given situation. She is obsessed with all things spooky and dark – funerals, vampires, séances, and the like. She wears only black and writes moody poetry. She's usually quiet and keeps to herself. Lucy has a way of mysteriously appearing out of nowhere, and try as they might, her siblings never get used to this.

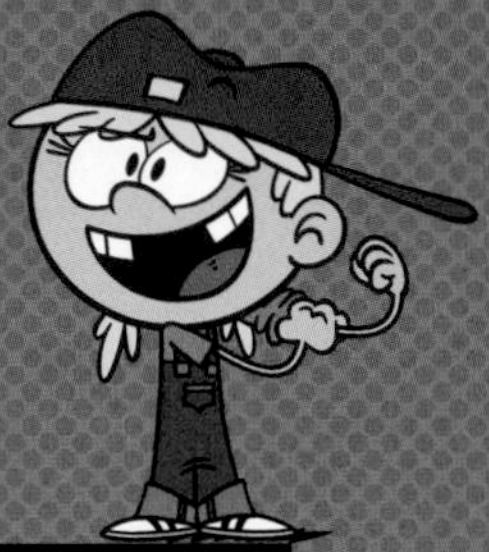

LANA LOUD
THE TOMBOY (6)

Lana is the rough-and-tumble sparkplug counterpart to her twin sister, Lola. She's all about reptiles, mud pies, and muffler repair. She's the resident Ms. Fix-it and is always ready to lend a hand – the dirtier the job, the better. Need your toilet unclogged? Snake fed? Back-zit popped? Lana's your gal. All she asks in return is a little A-B-C gum, or a handful of kibble (she often sneaks it from the dog bowl).

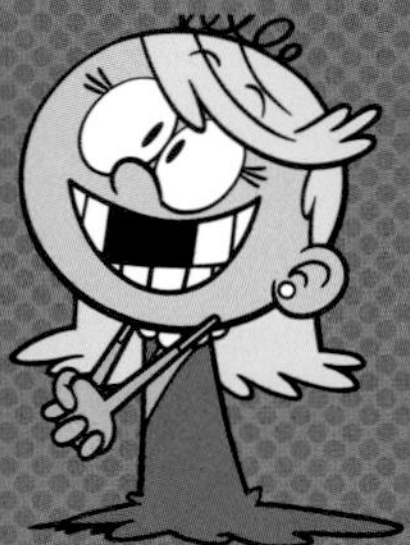

LOLA LOUD
THE BEAUTY QUEEN (6)

Lola could not be more different from her twin sister, Lana. She's a pageant powerhouse whose interests include glitter, photo shoots, and her own beautiful, beautiful face. But don't let her cute, toothless smile fool you; underneath all the sugar and spice lurks a Machiavellian mastermind. Whatever Lola wants, Lola gets – or else. She's the eyes and ears of the household and never resists an opportunity to tattle on troublemakers. But if you stay on Lola's good side, you've got yourself a fierce ally – and a lifetime supply of free makeovers.

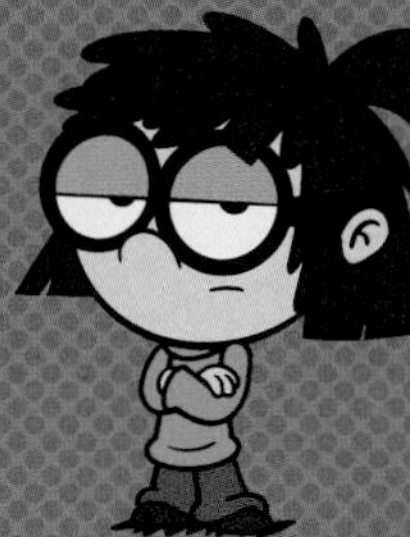

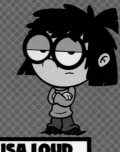

LISA LOUD
THE GENIUS (4)

Lisa is smarter than the rest of her siblings combined. She'll most likely be a rocket scientist, or a brain surgeon, or an evil genius who takes over the world. Lisa spends most of her time working in her lab (the family has gotten used to the explosions), and says her research leaves little time for frivolous human pursuits like "playing" or "getting haircuts." That said, she's always there to help with a homework question, or to explain why the sky is blue, or to point out the structural flaws in someone's pillow fort. Lisa says it's the least she can do for her favorite test subjects, er, siblings.

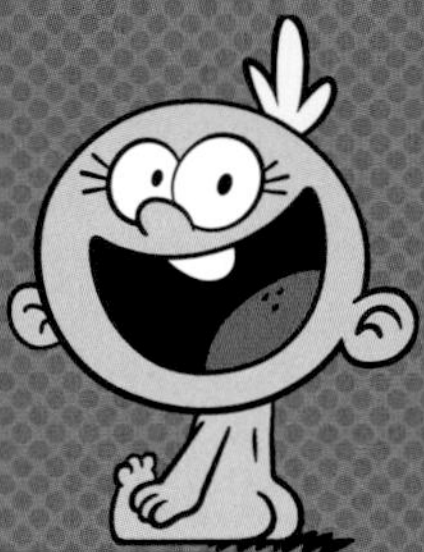

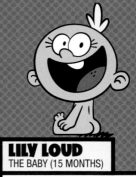

LILY LOUD
THE BABY (15 MONTHS)

Lily is a giggly, drooly, diaper-ditching free spirit, affectionately known as "the poop machine." You can't keep a nappy on this kid – she's like a teething Houdini. But even when Lily's running wild, dropping rancid diaper bombs, or drooling all over the remote, she always brings a smile to everyone's face (and a clothespin to their nose). Lily is everyone's favorite little buddy, and the whole family loves her unconditionally.

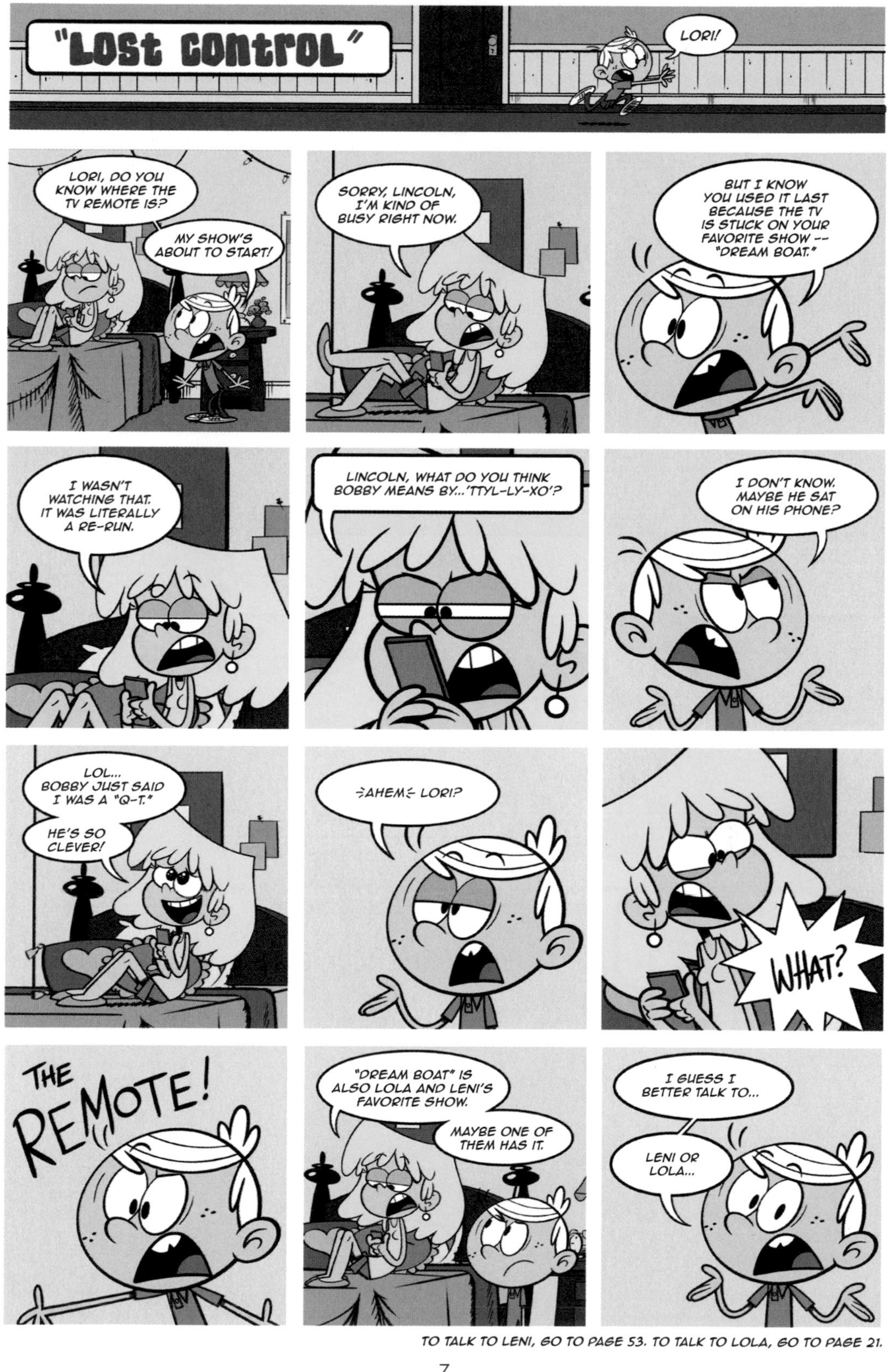
"LOST CONTROL"
LORI!
LORI, DO YOU KNOW WHERE THE TV REMOTE IS?
MY SHOW'S ABOUT TO START!
SORRY, LINCOLN, I'M KIND OF BUSY RIGHT NOW.
BUT I KNOW YOU USED IT LAST BECAUSE THE TV IS STUCK ON YOUR FAVORITE SHOW -- "DREAM BOAT."
I WASN'T WATCHING THAT. IT WAS LITERALLY A RE-RUN.
LINCOLN, WHAT DO YOU THINK BOBBY MEANS BY...'TTYL-LY-XO'?
I DON'T KNOW. MAYBE HE SAT ON HIS PHONE?
LOL... BOBBY JUST SAID I WAS A "Q-T."
HE'S SO CLEVER!
AHEM LORI?
WHAT?
THE REMOTE!
"DREAM BOAT" IS ALSO LOLA AND LENI'S FAVORITE SHOW.
MAYBE ONE OF THEM HAS IT.
I GUESS I BETTER TALK TO...
LENI OR LOLA...

TO TALK TO LENI, GO TO PAGE 53. TO TALK TO LOLA, GO TO PAGE 21.

"NO, YOU HANG UP"

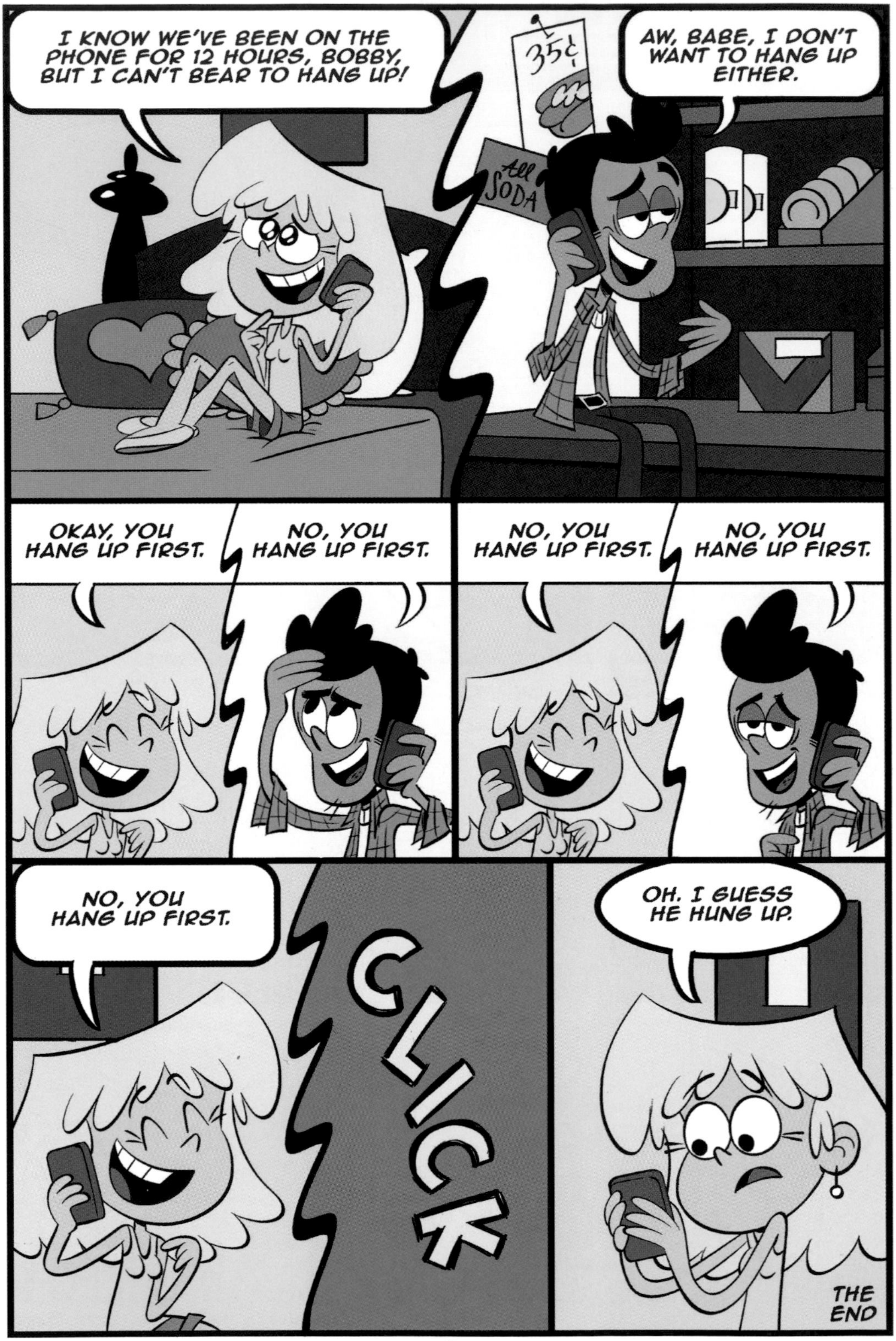

I KNOW WE'VE BEEN ON THE PHONE FOR 12 HOURS, BOBBY, BUT I CAN'T BEAR TO HANG UP!
35¢
All SODA
AW, BABE, I DON'T WANT TO HANG UP EITHER.
OKAY, YOU HANG UP FIRST.
NO, YOU HANG UP FIRST.
NO, YOU HANG UP FIRST.
NO, YOU HANG UP FIRST.
NO, YOU HANG UP FIRST.
CLICK
OH. I GUESS HE HUNG UP.
THE END

"THE HANDSHAKE"

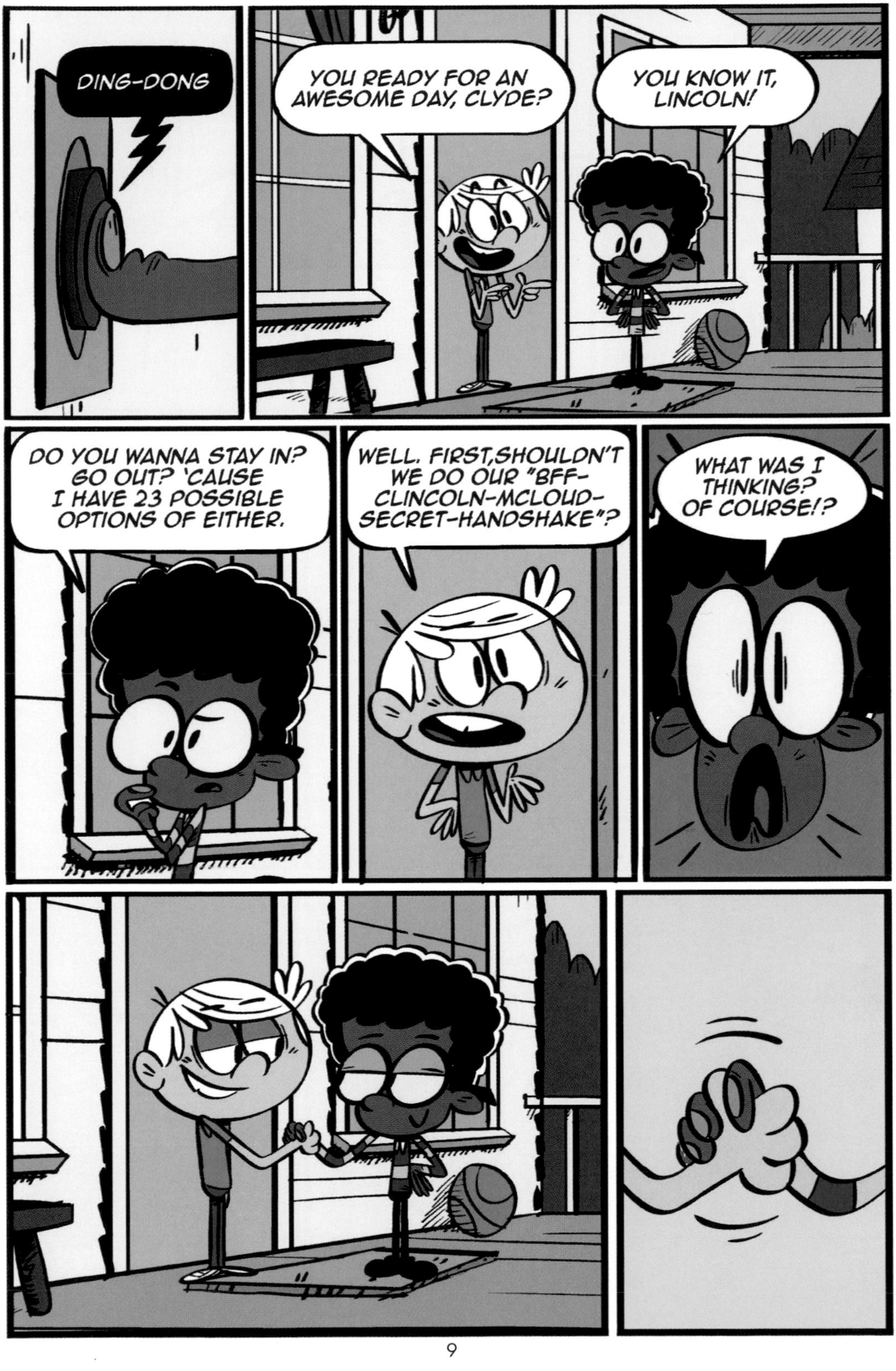
DING-DONG
YOU READY FOR AN AWESOME DAY, CLYDE?
YOU KNOW IT, LINCOLN!
DO YOU WANNA STAY IN? GO OUT? 'CAUSE I HAVE 23 POSSIBLE OPTIONS OF EITHER.
WELL. FIRST,SHOULDN'T WE DO OUR "BFF-CLINCOLN-MCLOUD-SECRET-HANDSHAKE"?
WHAT WAS I THINKING? OF COURSE!?

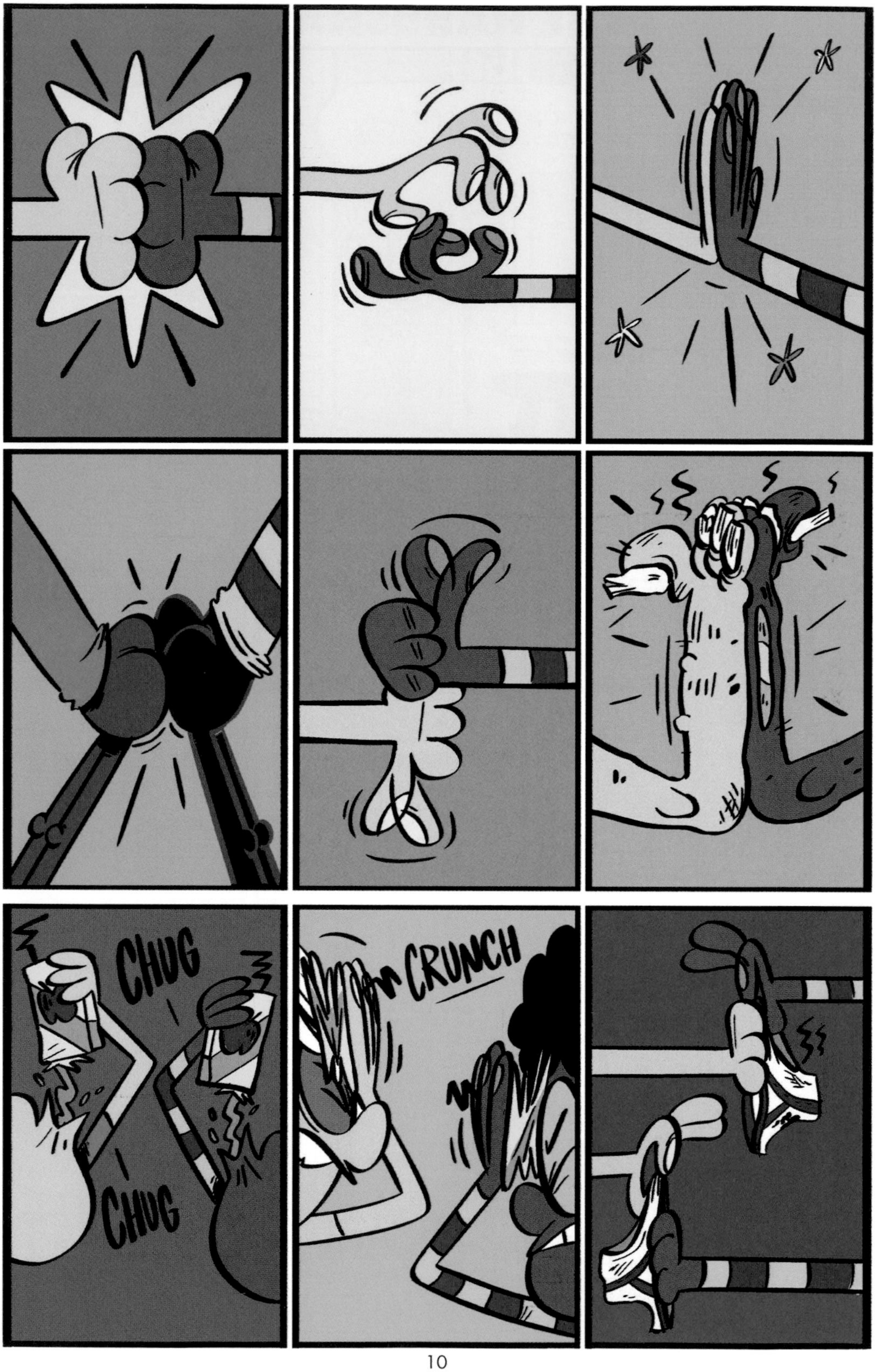
CHUG
CHUG
CRUNCH

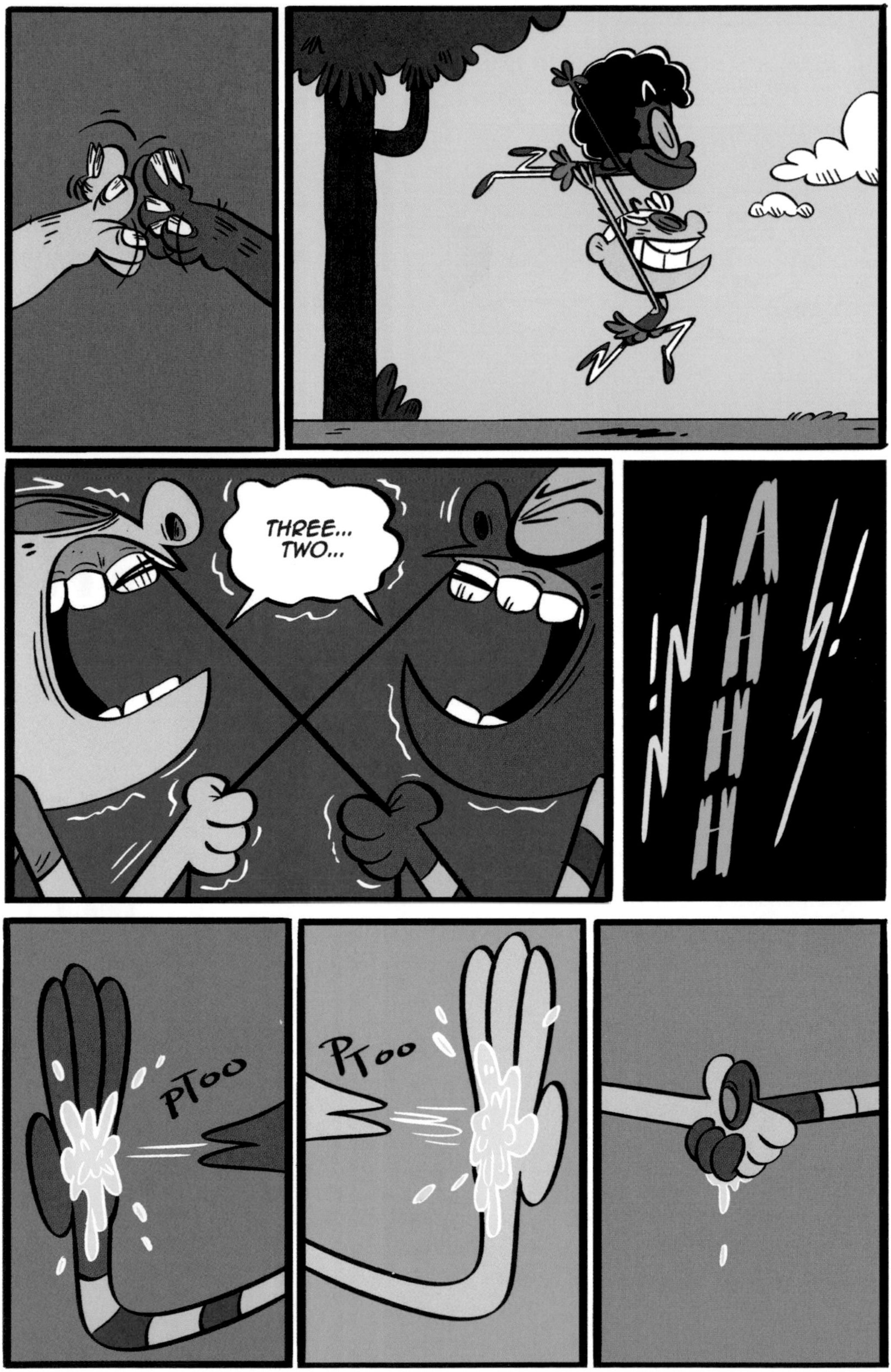
THREE... TWO...
AAHHHHH!
PTOO
PTOO

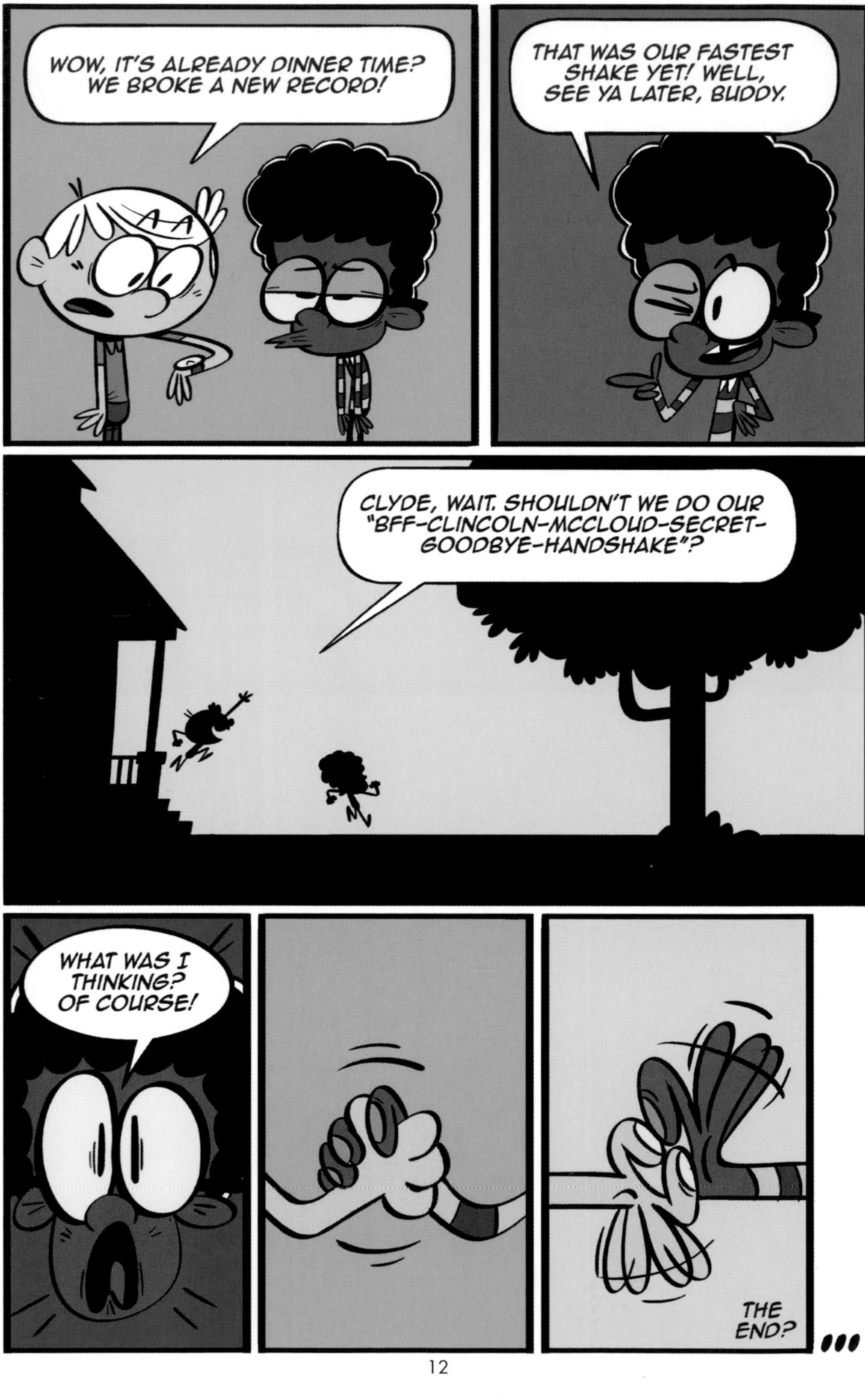
WOW, IT'S ALREADY DINNER TIME? WE BROKE A NEW RECORD!
THAT WAS OUR FASTEST SHAKE YET! WELL, SEE YA LATER, BUDDY.
CLYDE, WAIT. SHOULDN'T WE DO OUR "BFF-CLINCOLN-MCCLOUD-SECRET-GOODBYE-HANDSHAKE"?
WHAT WAS I THINKING? OF COURSE!
THE END?

"LUNA'S NEW THREADS"

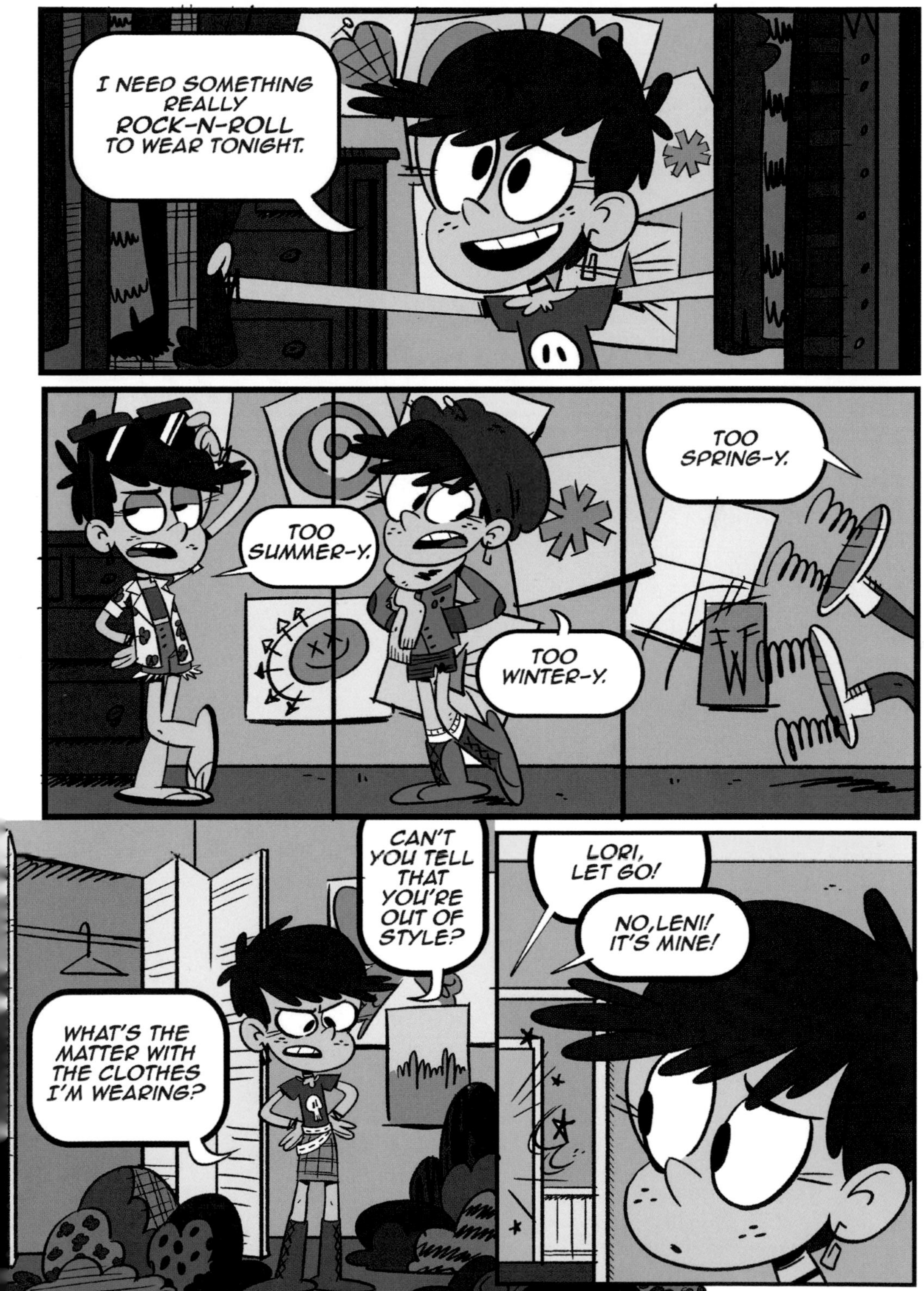
I NEED SOMETHING REALLY ROCK-N-ROLL TO WEAR TONIGHT.
TOO SUMMER-Y.
TOO WINTER-Y.
TOO SPRING-Y.
CAN'T YOU TELL THAT YOU'RE OUT OF STYLE?
WHAT'S THE MATTER WITH THE CLOTHES I'M WEARING?
LORI, LET GO!
NO,LENI! IT'S MINE!

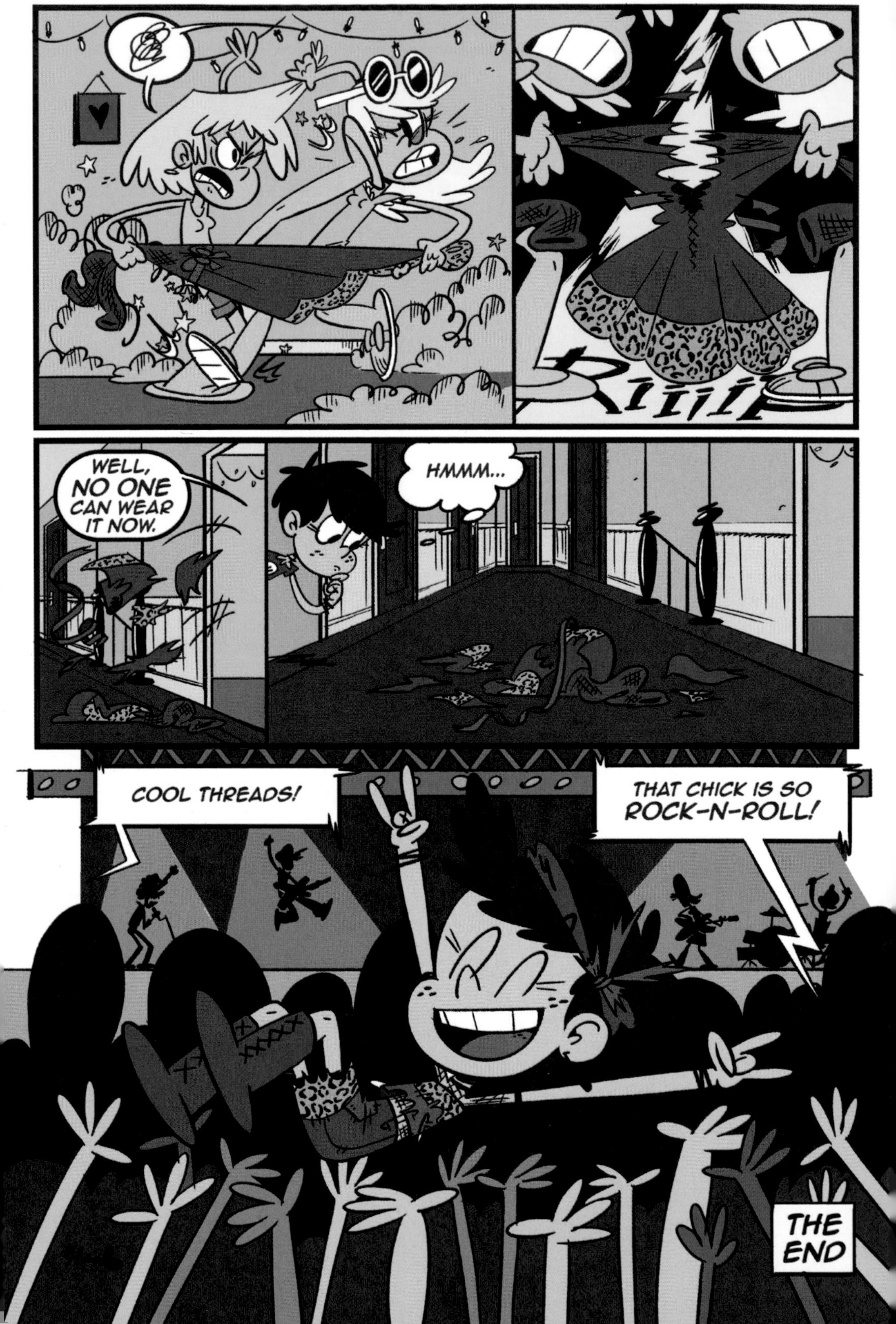
RIIIIIP
WELL, NO ONE CAN WEAR IT NOW.
HMMM...
COOL THREADS!
THAT CHICK IS SO ROCK-N-ROLL!
THE END

"VIDEO GAME MOJO"

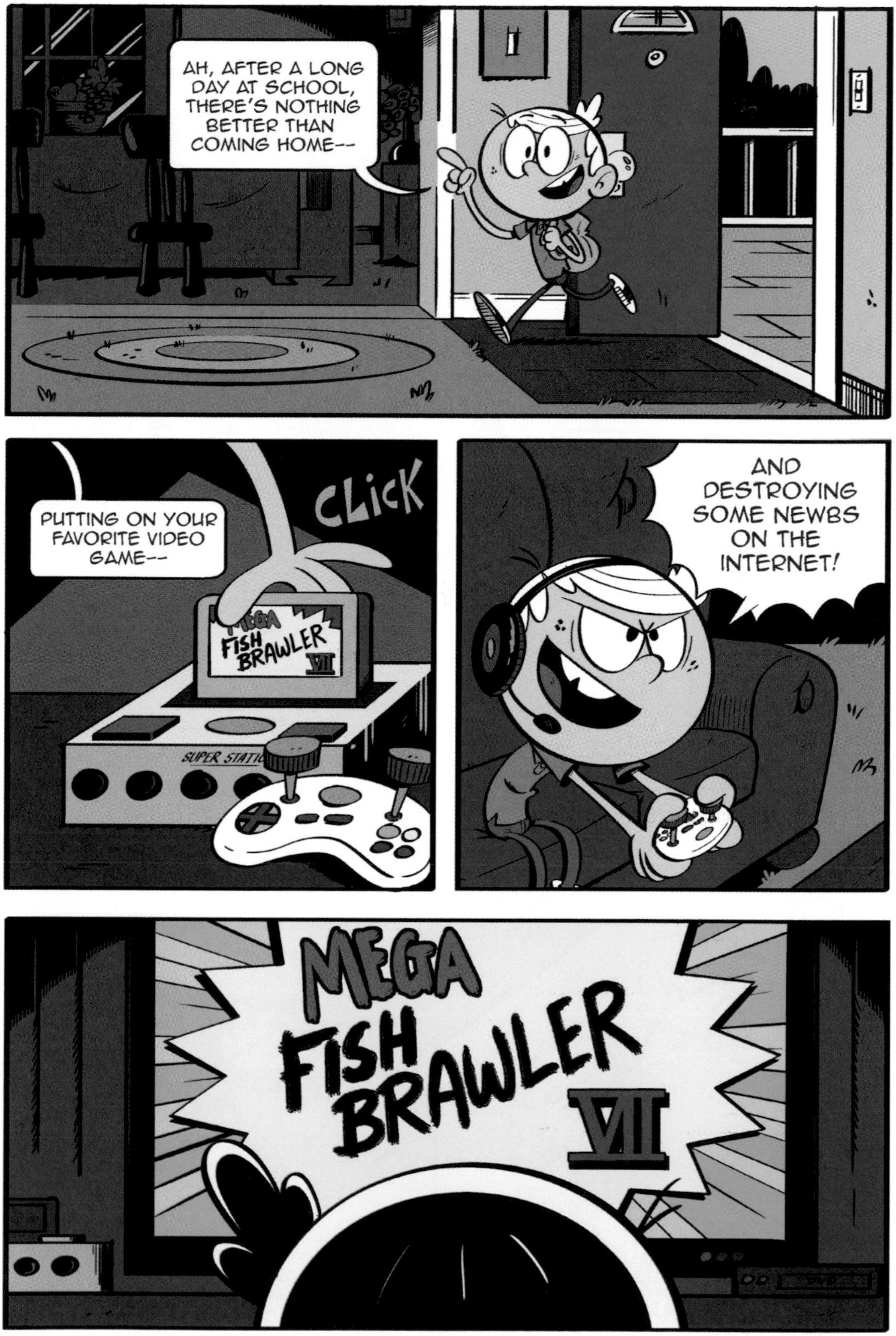

AH, AFTER A LONG DAY AT SCHOOL, THERE'S NOTHING BETTER THAN COMING HOME--
PUTTING ON YOUR FAVORITE VIDEO GAME--
CLICK
MEGA FISH BRAWLER VII
AND DESTROYING SOME NEWBS ON THE INTERNET!
MEGA FISH BRAWLER VII

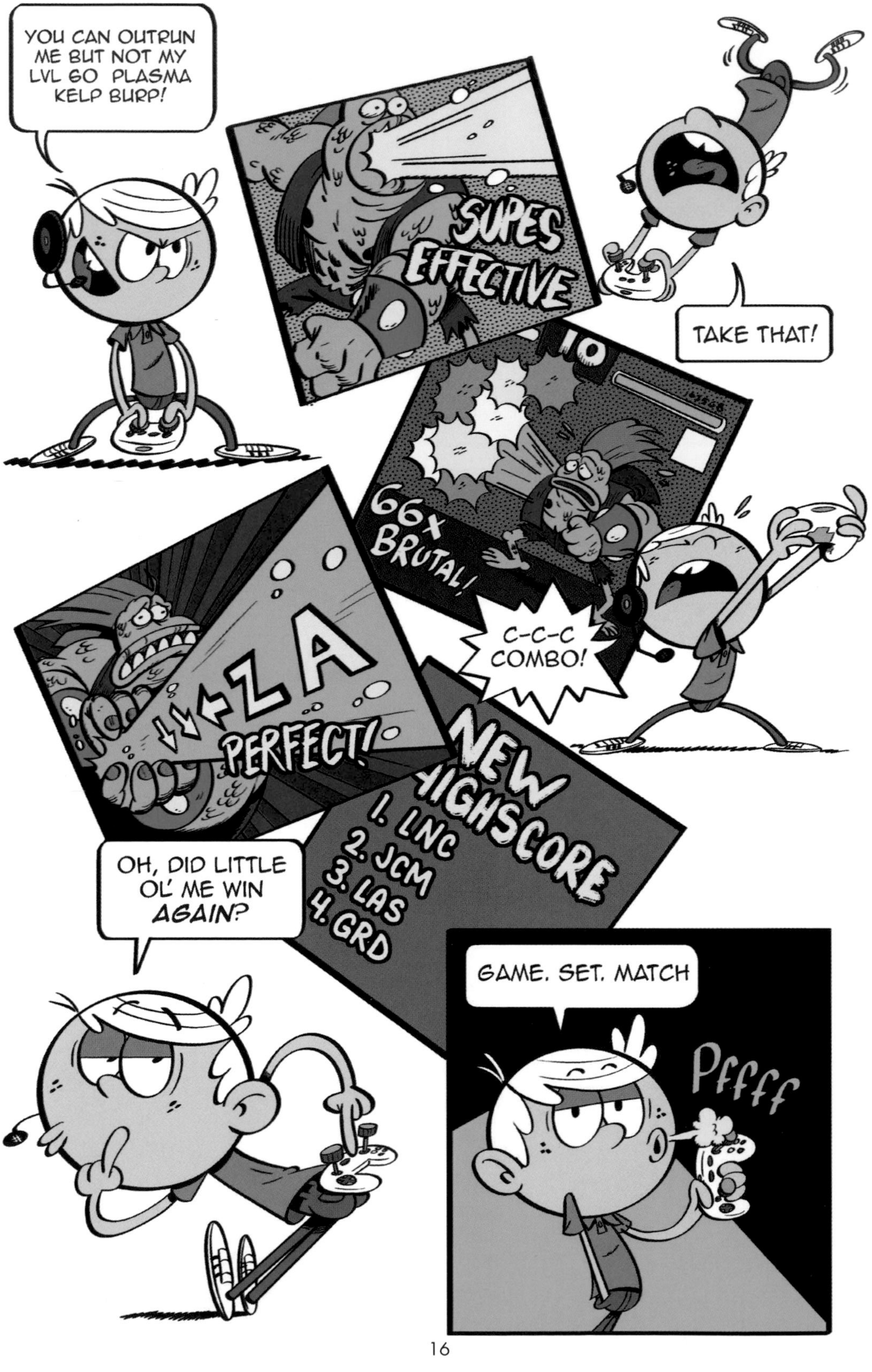
YOU CAN OUTRUN ME BUT NOT MY LVL 60 PLASMA KELP BURP!
SUPES EFFECTIVE
TAKE THAT!
10
66x BRUTAL!
C-C-C COMBO!
ZA
PERFECT!
NEW HIGHSCORE
1. LNC
2. JCM
3. LAS
4. GRD
OH, DID LITTLE OL' ME WIN AGAIN?
GAME. SET. MATCH
Pffff

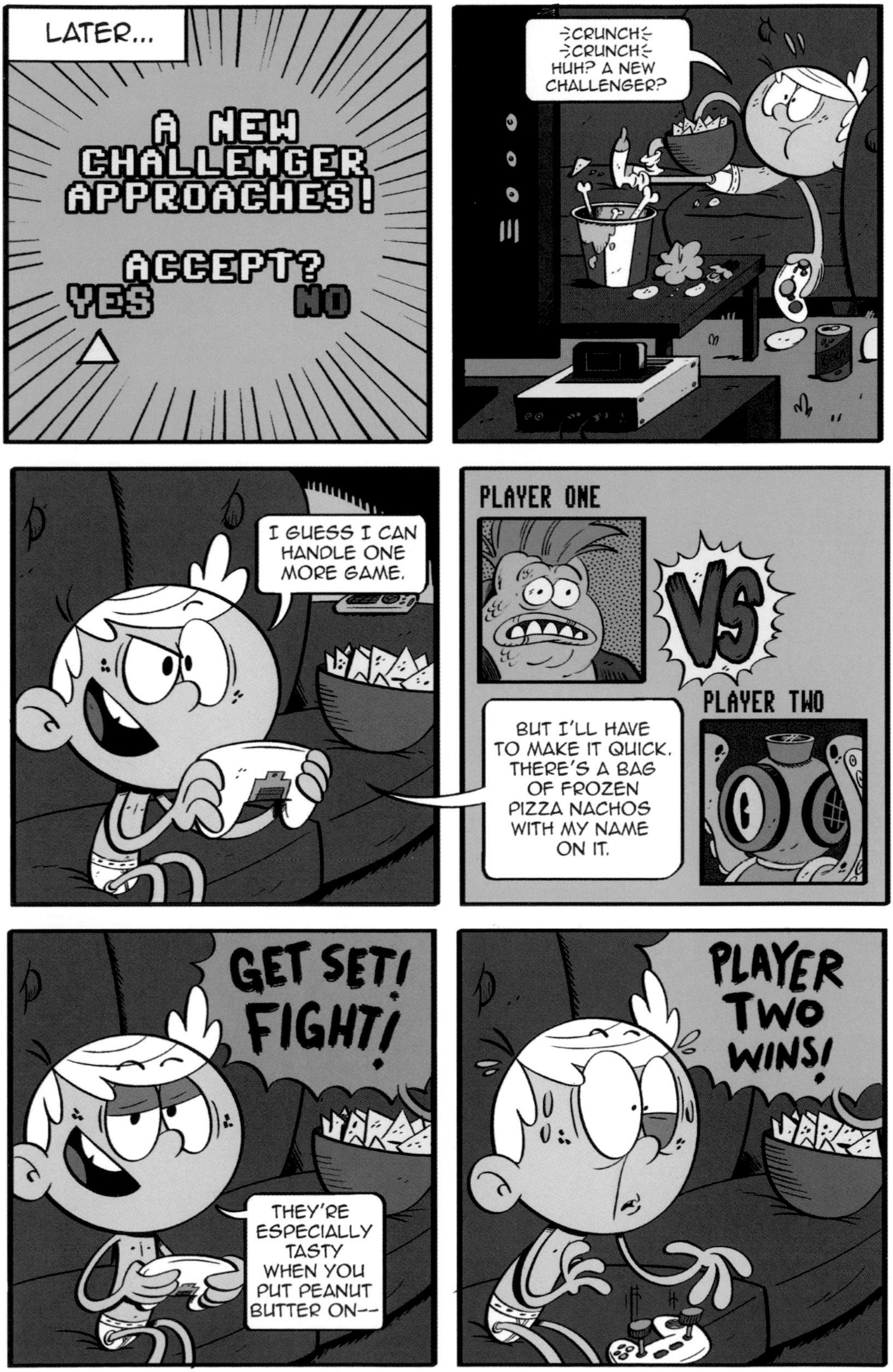

LATER...
A NEW CHALLENGER APPROACHES!
ACCEPT?
YES
NO
CRUNCH CRUNCH HUH? A NEW CHALLENGER?
I GUESS I CAN HANDLE ONE MORE GAME.
PLAYER ONE
VS
PLAYER TWO
BUT I'LL HAVE TO MAKE IT QUICK. THERE'S A BAG OF FROZEN PIZZA NACHOS WITH MY NAME ON IT.
GET SET! FIGHT!
THEY'RE ESPECIALLY TASTY WHEN YOU PUT PEANUT BUTTER ON--
PLAYER TWO WINS!

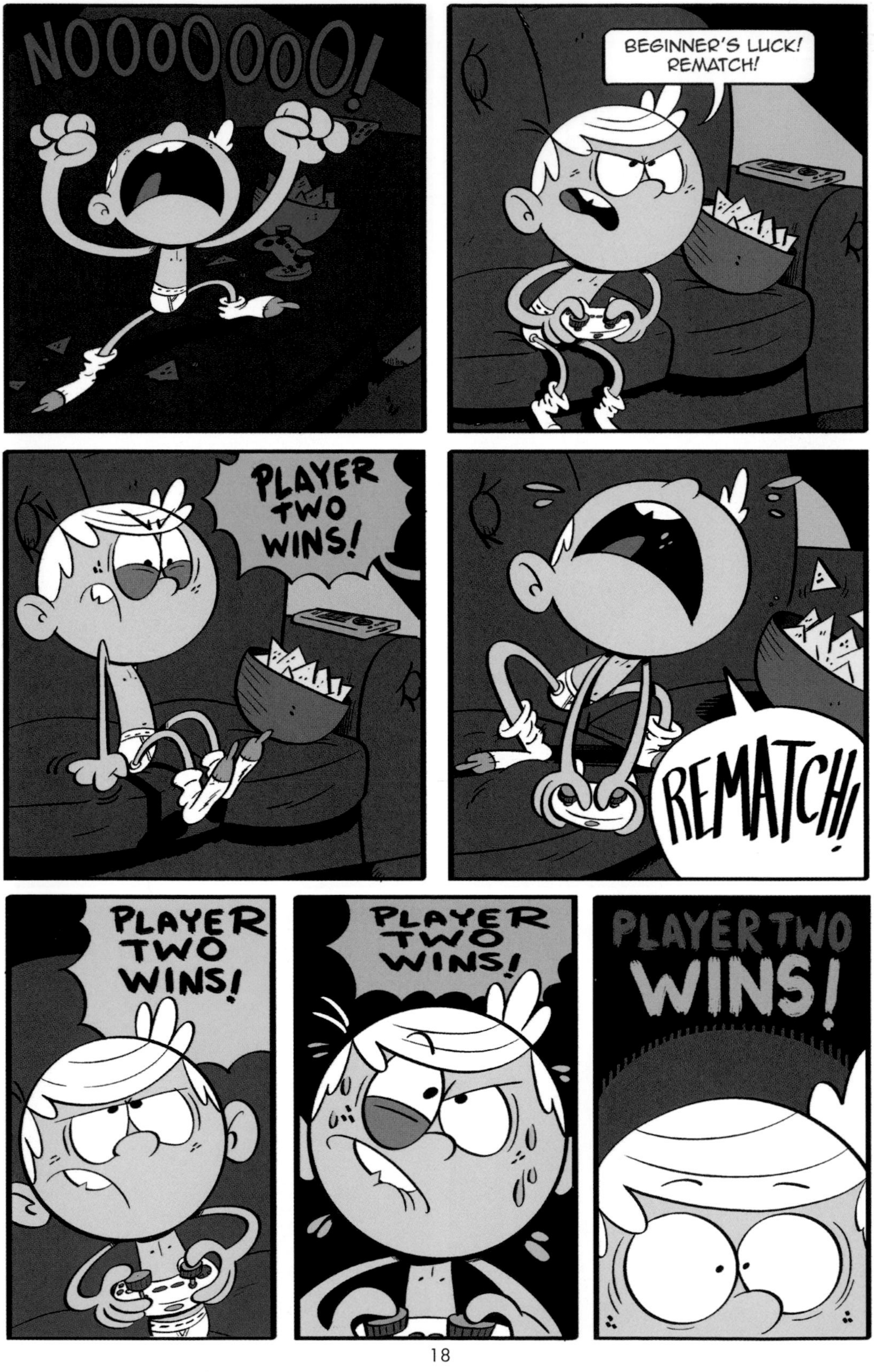
NOOOOOOO!
BEGINNER'S LUCK! REMATCH!
PLAYER TWO WINS!
REMATCH!
PLAYER TWO WINS!
PLAYER TWO WINS!
PLAYER TWO WINS!

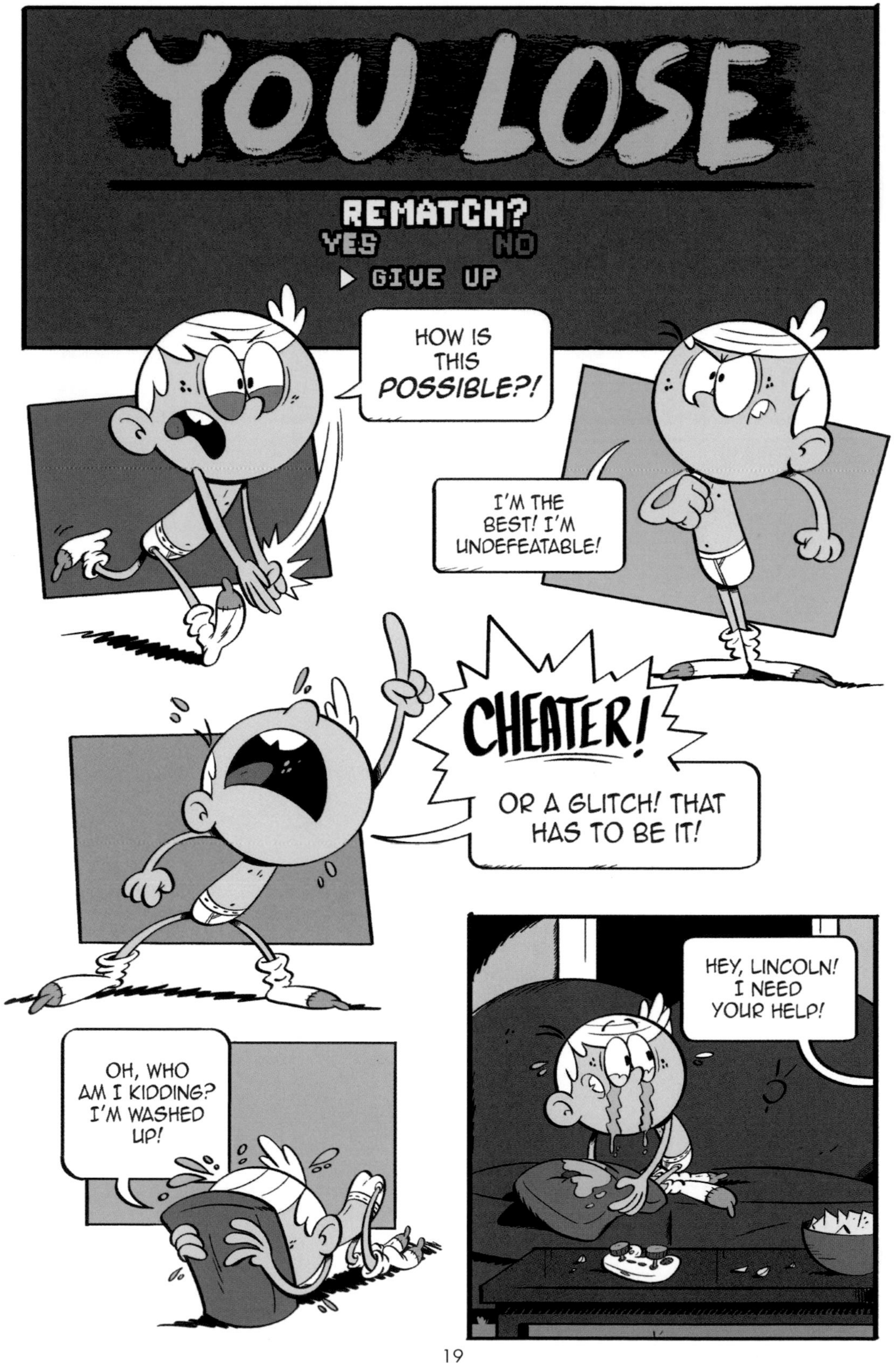
YOU LOSE
REMATCH?
YES
NO
GIVE UP
HOW IS THIS *POSSIBLE?!*
I'M THE BEST! I'M UNDEFEATABLE!
CHEATER!
OR A GLITCH! THAT HAS TO BE IT!
OH, WHO AM I KIDDING? I'M WASHED UP!
HEY, LINCOLN! I NEED YOUR HELP!

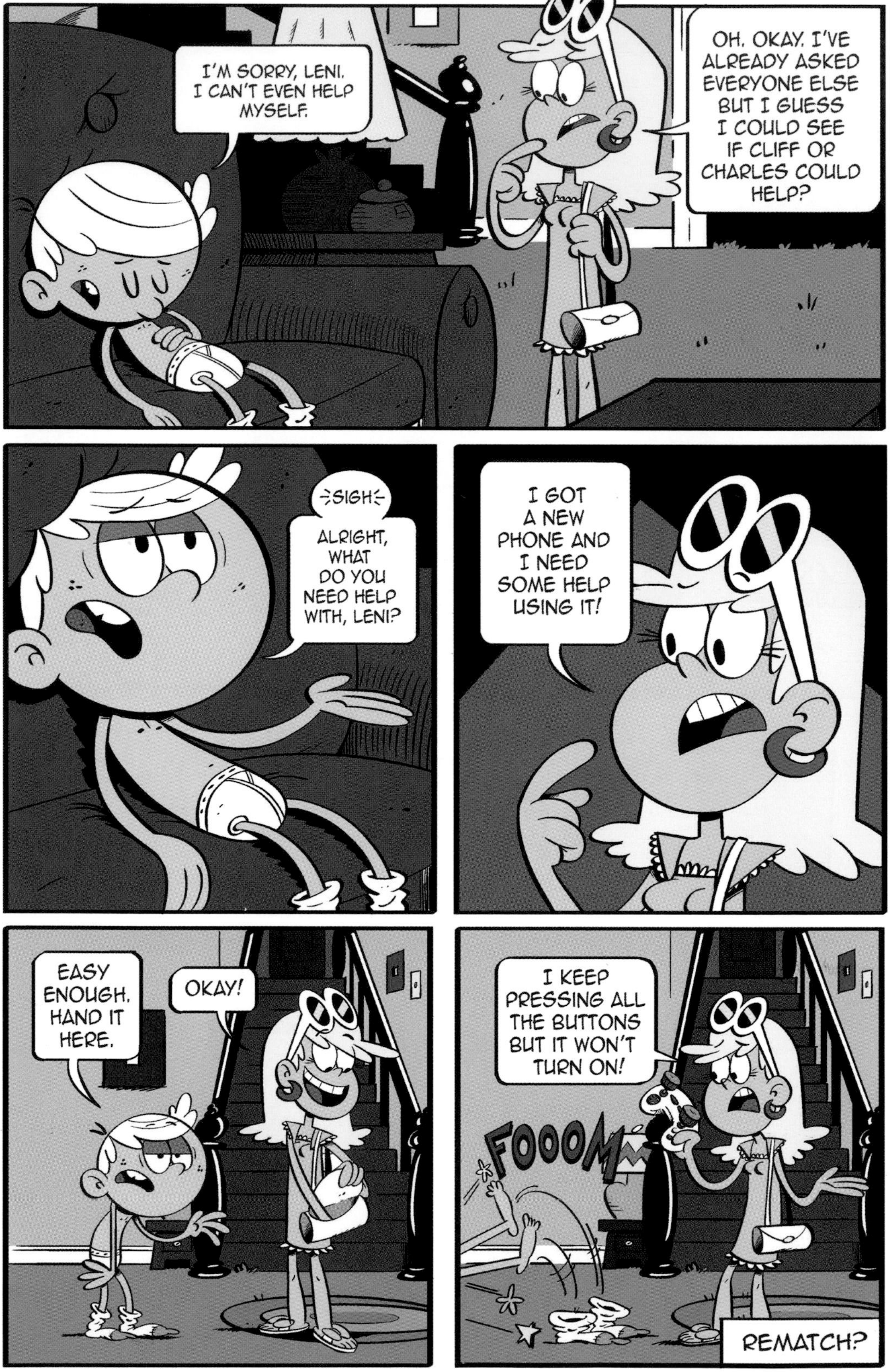
I'M SORRY, LENI. I CAN'T EVEN HELP MYSELF.
OH. OKAY. I'VE ALREADY ASKED EVERYONE ELSE BUT I GUESS I COULD SEE IF CLIFF OR CHARLES COULD HELP?
SIGH
ALRIGHT, WHAT DO YOU NEED HELP WITH, LENI?
I GOT A NEW PHONE AND I NEED SOME HELP USING IT!
EASY ENOUGH. HAND IT HERE.
OKAY!
I KEEP PRESSING ALL THE BUTTONS BUT IT WON'T TURN ON!
FOOOM
REMATCH?

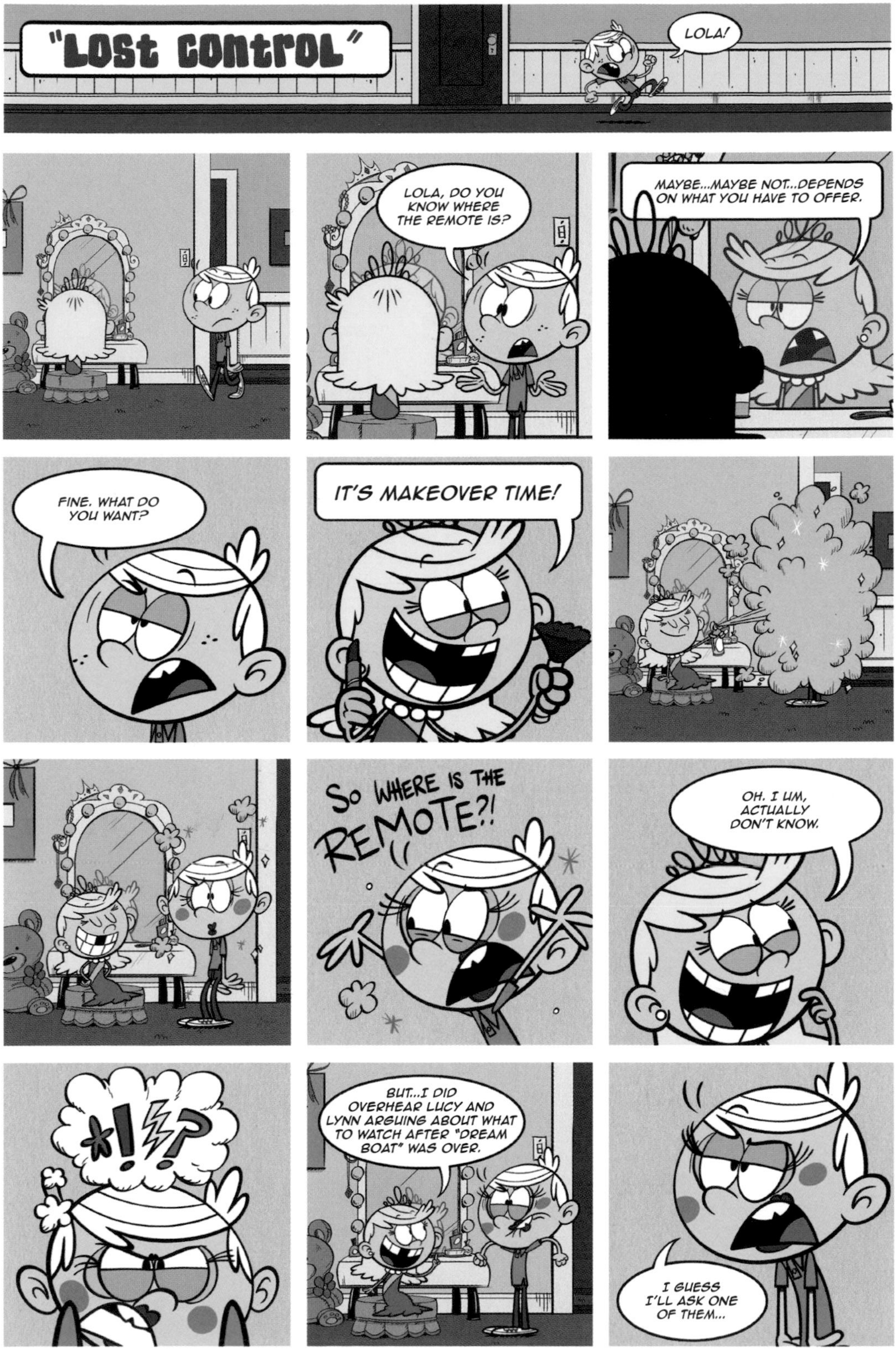
"LOST CONTROL"
LOLA!
LOLA, DO YOU KNOW WHERE THE REMOTE IS?
MAYBE...MAYBE NOT...DEPENDS ON WHAT YOU HAVE TO OFFER.
FINE. WHAT DO YOU WANT?
IT'S MAKEOVER TIME!
SO WHERE IS THE REMOTE?!
OH. I UM, ACTUALLY DON'T KNOW.
BUT...I DID OVERHEAR LUCY AND LYNN ARGUING ABOUT WHAT TO WATCH AFTER "DREAM BOAT" WAS OVER.
I GUESS I'LL ASK ONE OF THEM...

TO TALK TO LUCY, GO TO PAGE 25. TO TALK TO LYNN, GO TO PAGE 29.

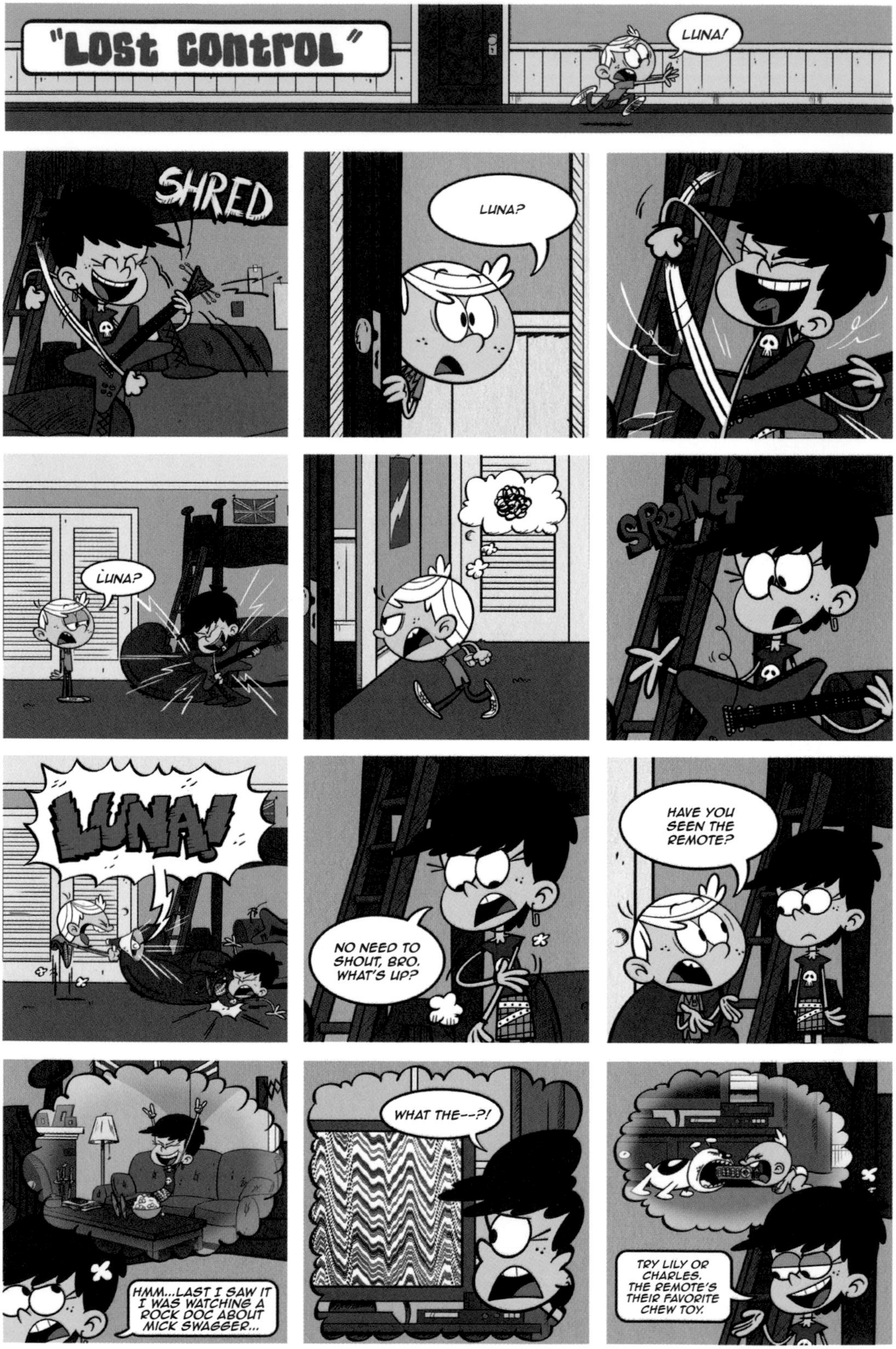
"LOST CONTROL"
LUNA!
SHRED
LUNA?
LUNA?
SPROING
LUNA!
NO NEED TO SHOUT, BRO. WHAT'S UP?
HAVE YOU SEEN THE REMOTE?
HMM...LAST I SAW IT I WAS WATCHING A ROCK DOC ABOUT MICK SWAGGER...
WHAT THE--?!
TRY LILY OR CHARLES. THE REMOTE'S THEIR FAVORITE CHEW TOY.

TO TALK TO LILY, GO TO PAGE 34. TO TALK TO CHARLES, GO TO PAGE 32.

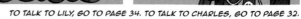

"GONE FISHING"

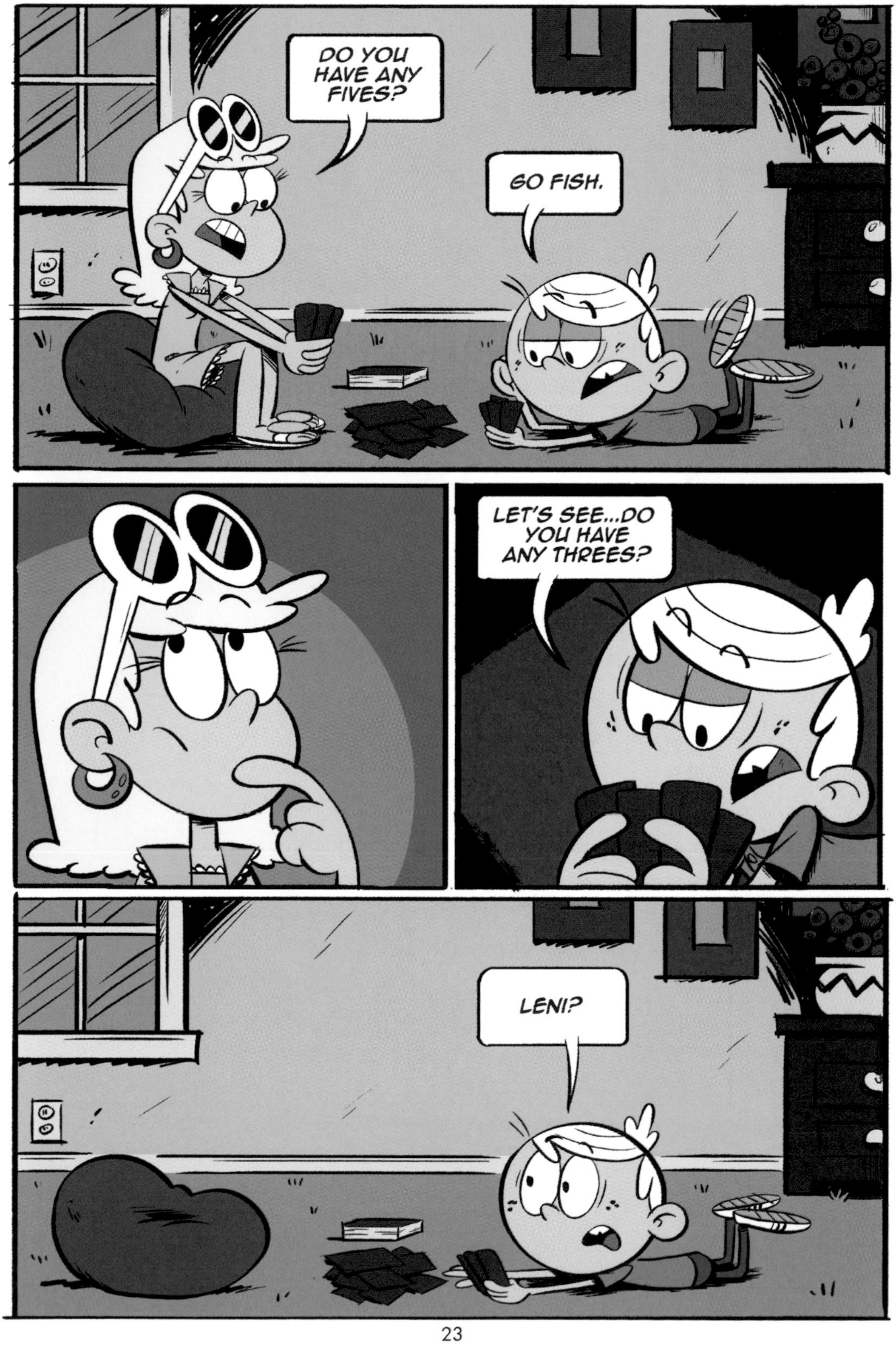
DO YOU HAVE ANY FIVES?
GO FISH.
LET'S SEE...DO YOU HAVE ANY THREES?
LENI?

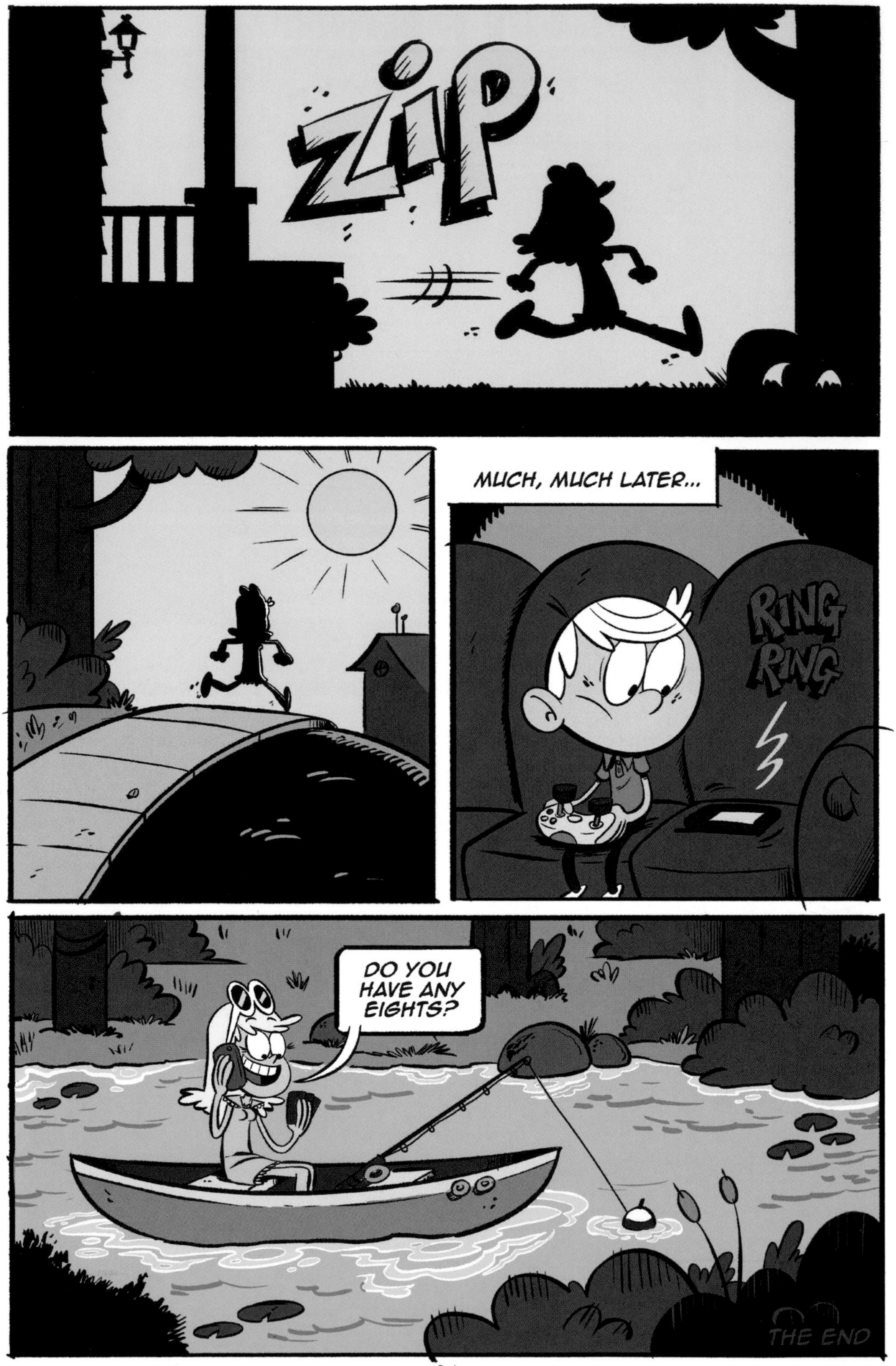
ZIP
MUCH, MUCH LATER...
RING RING
DO YOU HAVE ANY EIGHTS?
THE END

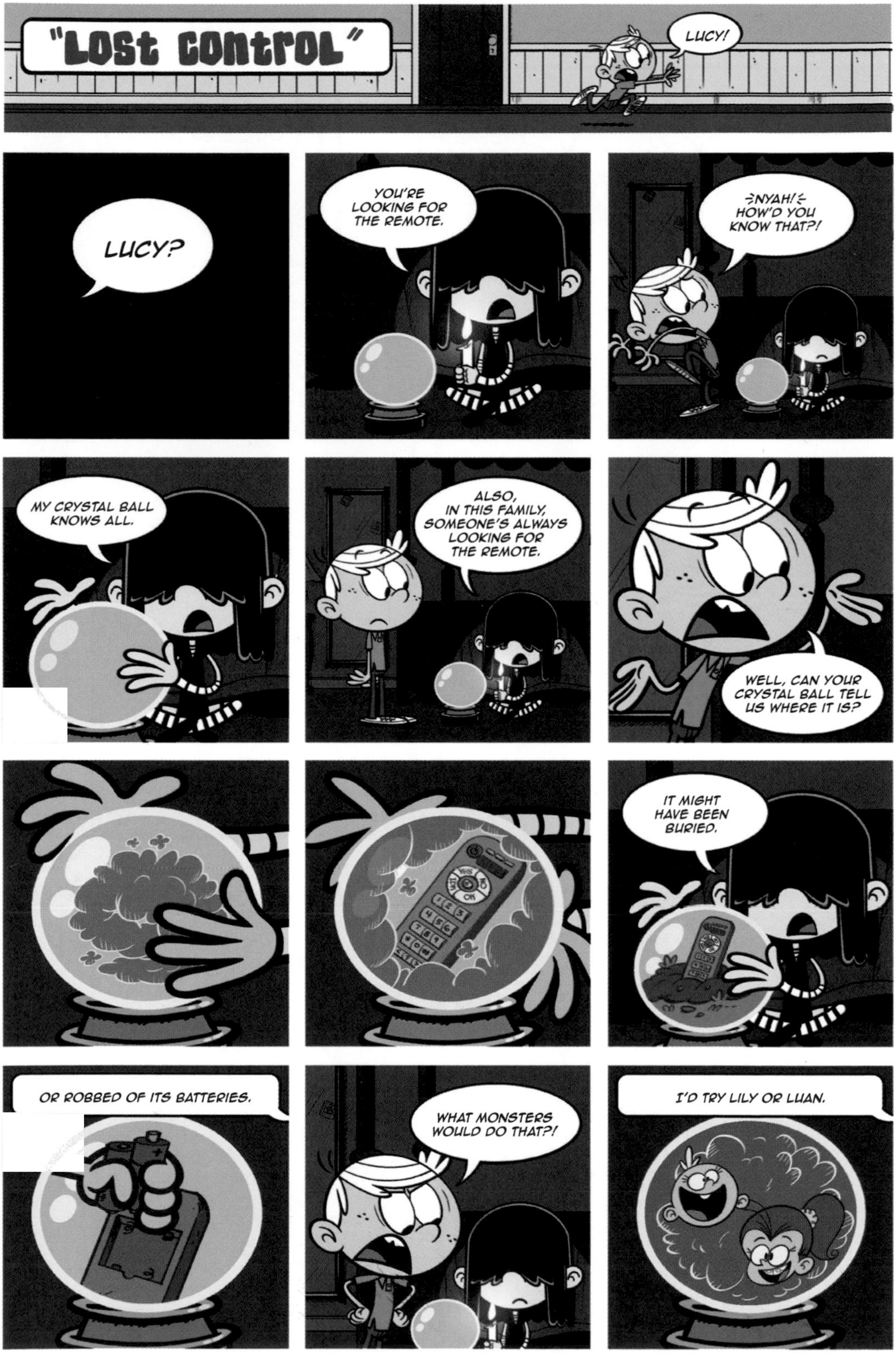
"LOST CONTROL"
LUCY!
LUCY?
YOU'RE LOOKING FOR THE REMOTE.
⇒NYAH!⇐ HOW'D YOU KNOW THAT?!
MY CRYSTAL BALL KNOWS ALL.
ALSO, IN THIS FAMILY, SOMEONE'S ALWAYS LOOKING FOR THE REMOTE.
WELL, CAN YOUR CRYSTAL BALL TELL US WHERE IT IS?
IT MIGHT HAVE BEEN BURIED.
OR ROBBED OF ITS BATTERIES.
WHAT MONSTERS WOULD DO THAT?!
I'D TRY LILY OR LUAN.

TO TALK TO LILY, GO TO PAGE 34. TO TALK TO LUAN, GO TO PAGE 35.

"LOUD AND ORDER"

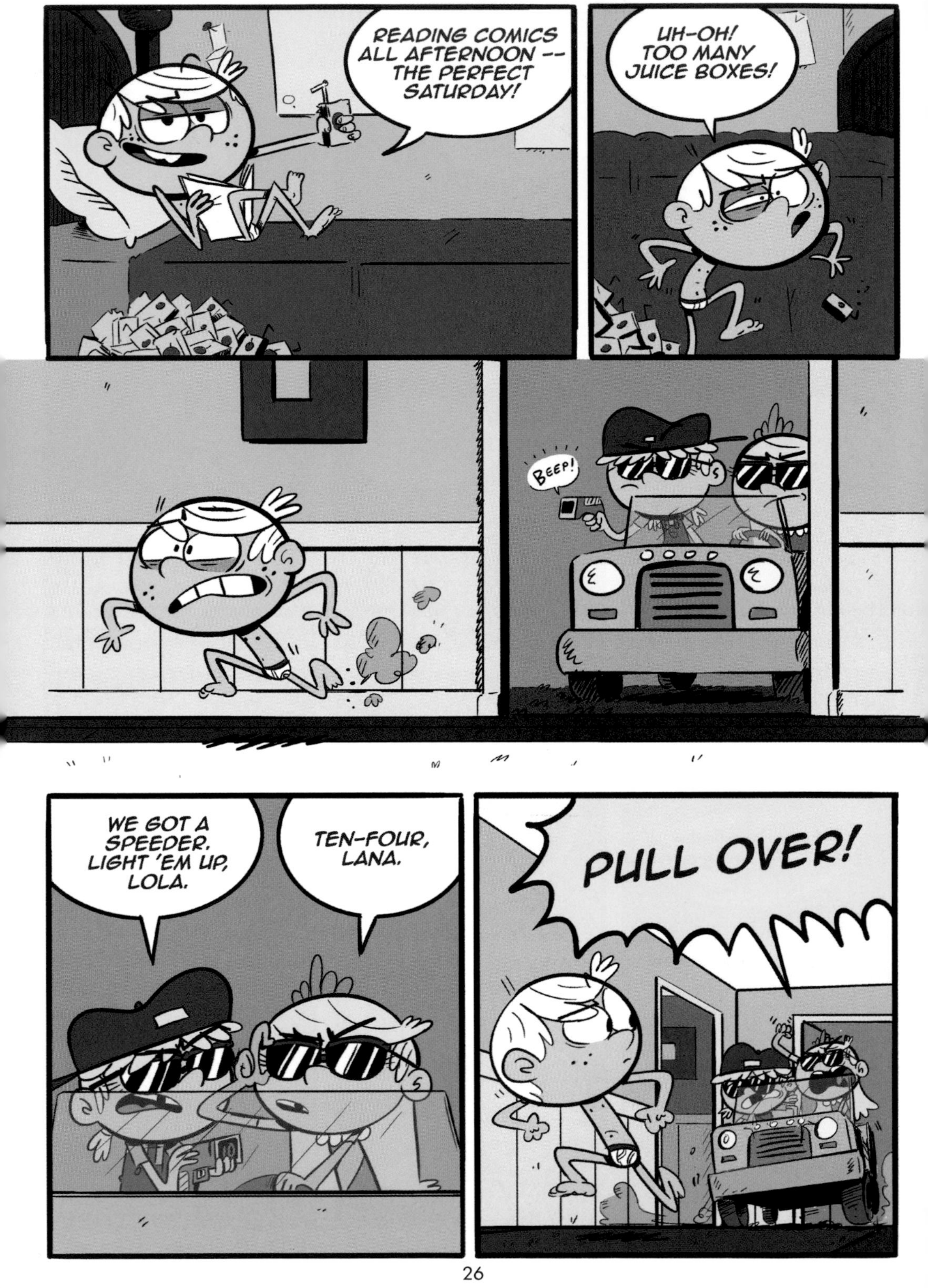
READING COMICS ALL AFTERNOON -- THE PERFECT SATURDAY!
UH-OH! TOO MANY JUICE BOXES!
BEEP!
WE GOT A SPEEDER. LIGHT 'EM UP, LOLA.
TEN-FOUR, LANA.
PULL OVER!

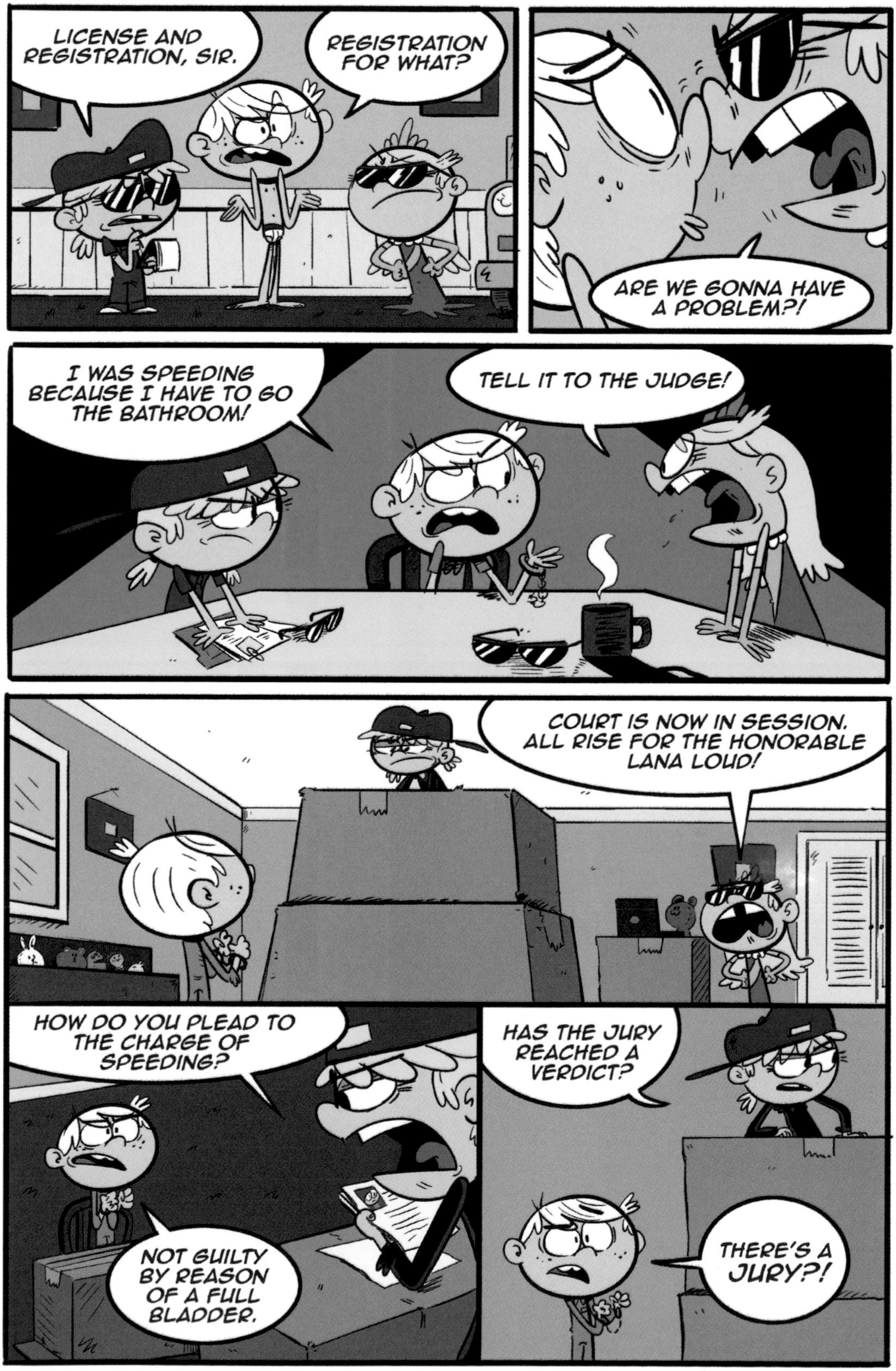

LICENSE AND REGISTRATION, SIR.
REGISTRATION FOR WHAT?
ARE WE GONNA HAVE A PROBLEM?!
I WAS SPEEDING BECAUSE I HAVE TO GO THE BATHROOM!
TELL IT TO THE JUDGE!
COURT IS NOW IN SESSION. ALL RISE FOR THE HONORABLE LANA LOUD!
HOW DO YOU PLEAD TO THE CHARGE OF SPEEDING?
NOT GUILTY BY REASON OF A FULL BLADDER.
HAS THE JURY REACHED A VERDICT?
THERE'S A JURY?!

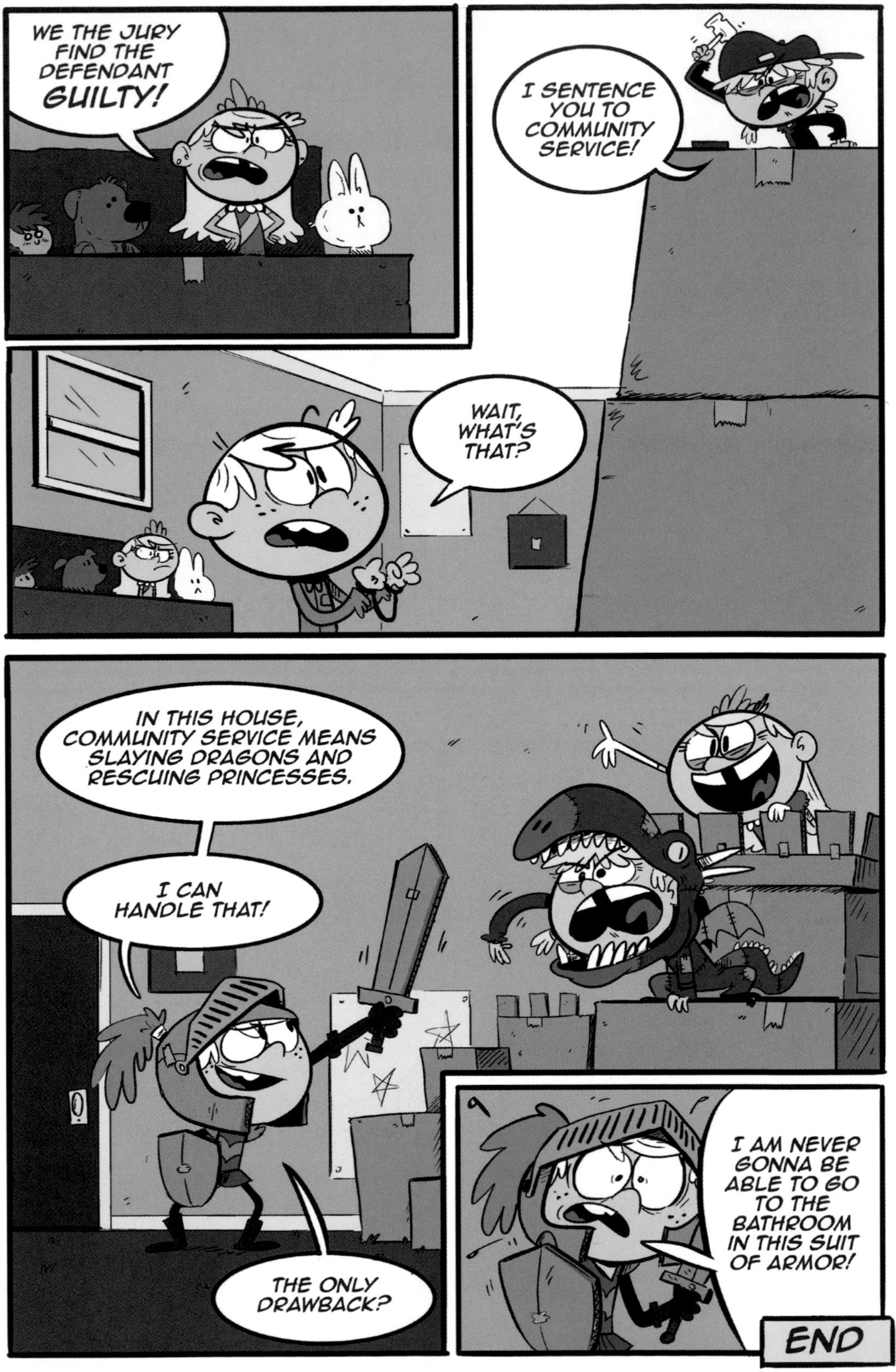

WE THE JURY FIND THE DEFENDANT GUILTY!
I SENTENCE YOU TO COMMUNITY SERVICE!
WAIT, WHAT'S THAT?
IN THIS HOUSE, COMMUNITY SERVICE MEANS SLAYING DRAGONS AND RESCUING PRINCESSES.
I CAN HANDLE THAT!
THE ONLY DRAWBACK?
I AM NEVER GONNA BE ABLE TO GO TO THE BATHROOM IN THIS SUIT OF ARMOR!
END

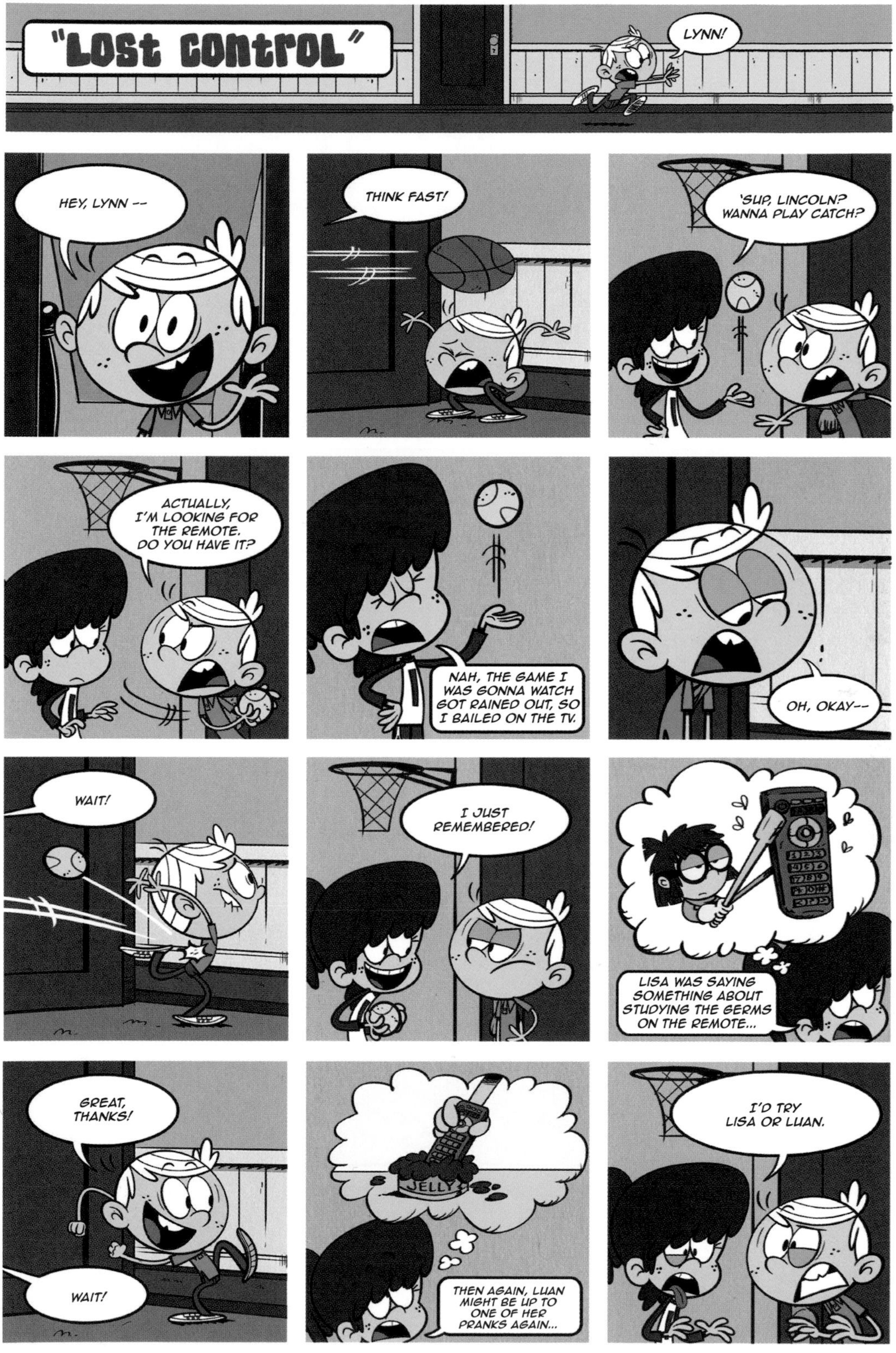
"LOST CONTROL"
LYNN!
HEY, LYNN --
THINK FAST!
'SUP, LINCOLN? WANNA PLAY CATCH?
ACTUALLY, I'M LOOKING FOR THE REMOTE. DO YOU HAVE IT?
NAH, THE GAME I WAS GONNA WATCH GOT RAINED OUT, SO I BAILED ON THE TV.
OH, OKAY--
WAIT!
I JUST REMEMBERED!
LISA WAS SAYING SOMETHING ABOUT STUDYING THE GERMS ON THE REMOTE...
GREAT, THANKS!
WAIT!
JELLY
THEN AGAIN, LUAN MIGHT BE UP TO ONE OF HER PRANKS AGAIN...
I'D TRY LISA OR LUAN.

TO TALK TO LISA, GO TO PAGE 40. TO TALK TO LUAN, GO TO PAGE 35.

"SHOCKER"

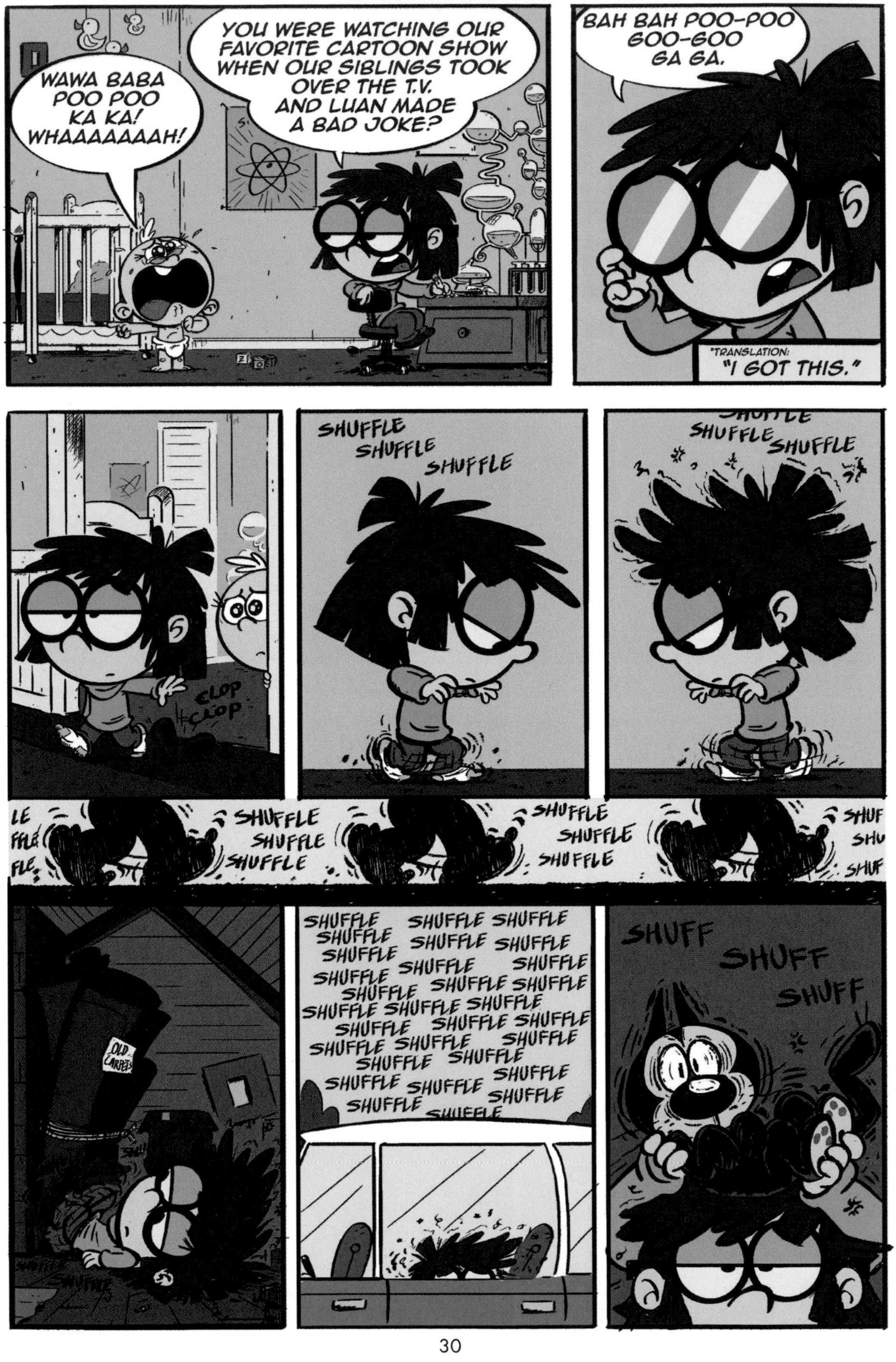

WAWA BABA POO POO KA KA! WHAAAAAAAAH!
YOU WERE WATCHING OUR FAVORITE CARTOON SHOW WHEN OUR SIBLINGS TOOK OVER THE T.V. AND LUAN MADE A BAD JOKE?
BAH BAH POO-POO GOO-GOO GA GA.
*TRANSLATION: "I GOT THIS."
CLOP CLOP
SHUFFLE SHUFFLE SHUFFLE
SHUFFLE SHUFFLE
SHUFFLE SHUFFLE SHUFFLE
SHUFFLE SHUFFLE SHUFFLE
OLD CARPETS
SHUFFLE SHUFFLE SHUFFLE
SHUFF SHUFF SHUFF

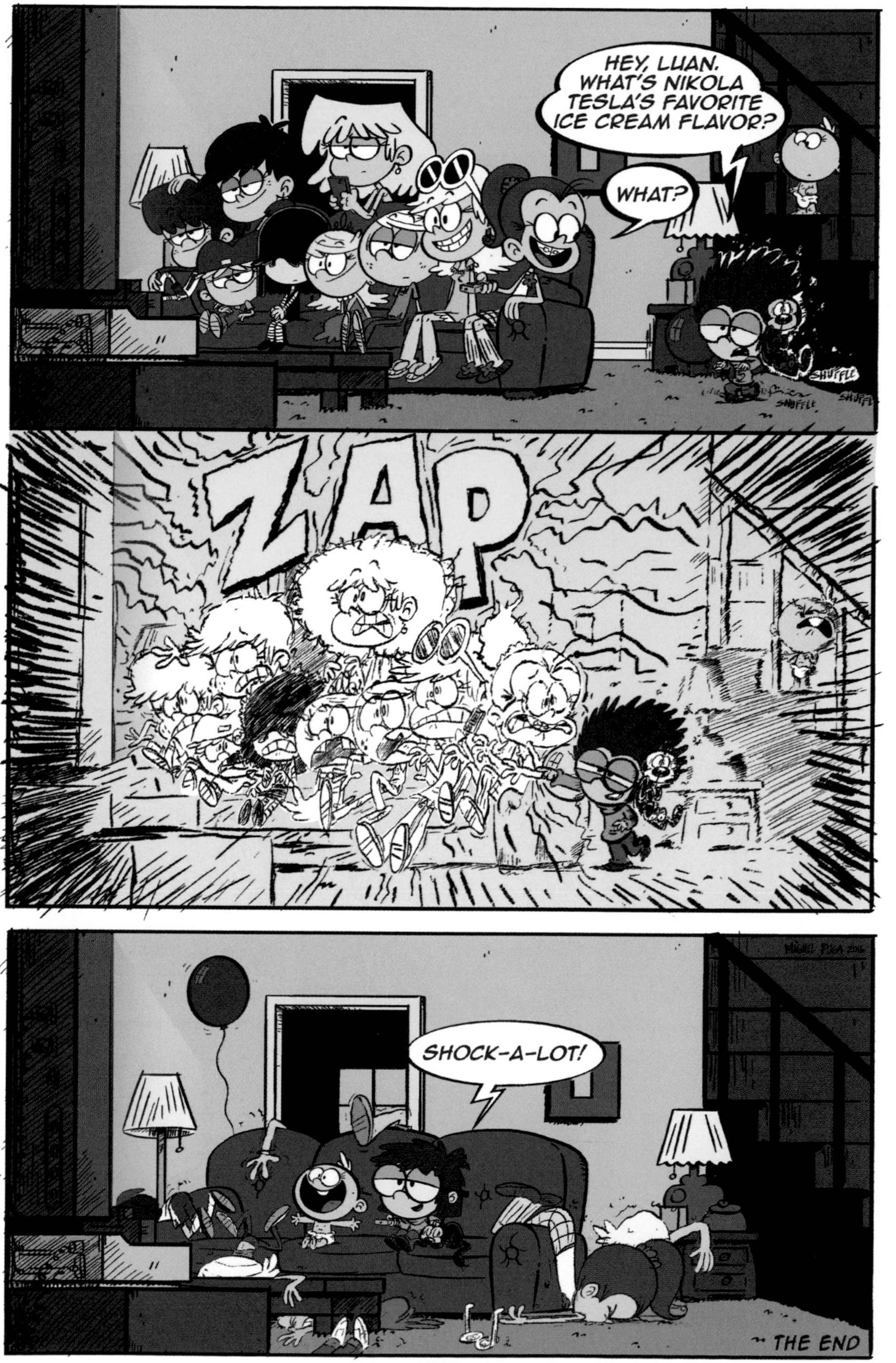
HEY, LUAN. WHAT'S NIKOLA TESLA'S FAVORITE ICE CREAM FLAVOR?
WHAT?
SHUFFLE
SHUFFLE
SHUFFLE
ZAP
SHOCK-A-LOT!
THE END

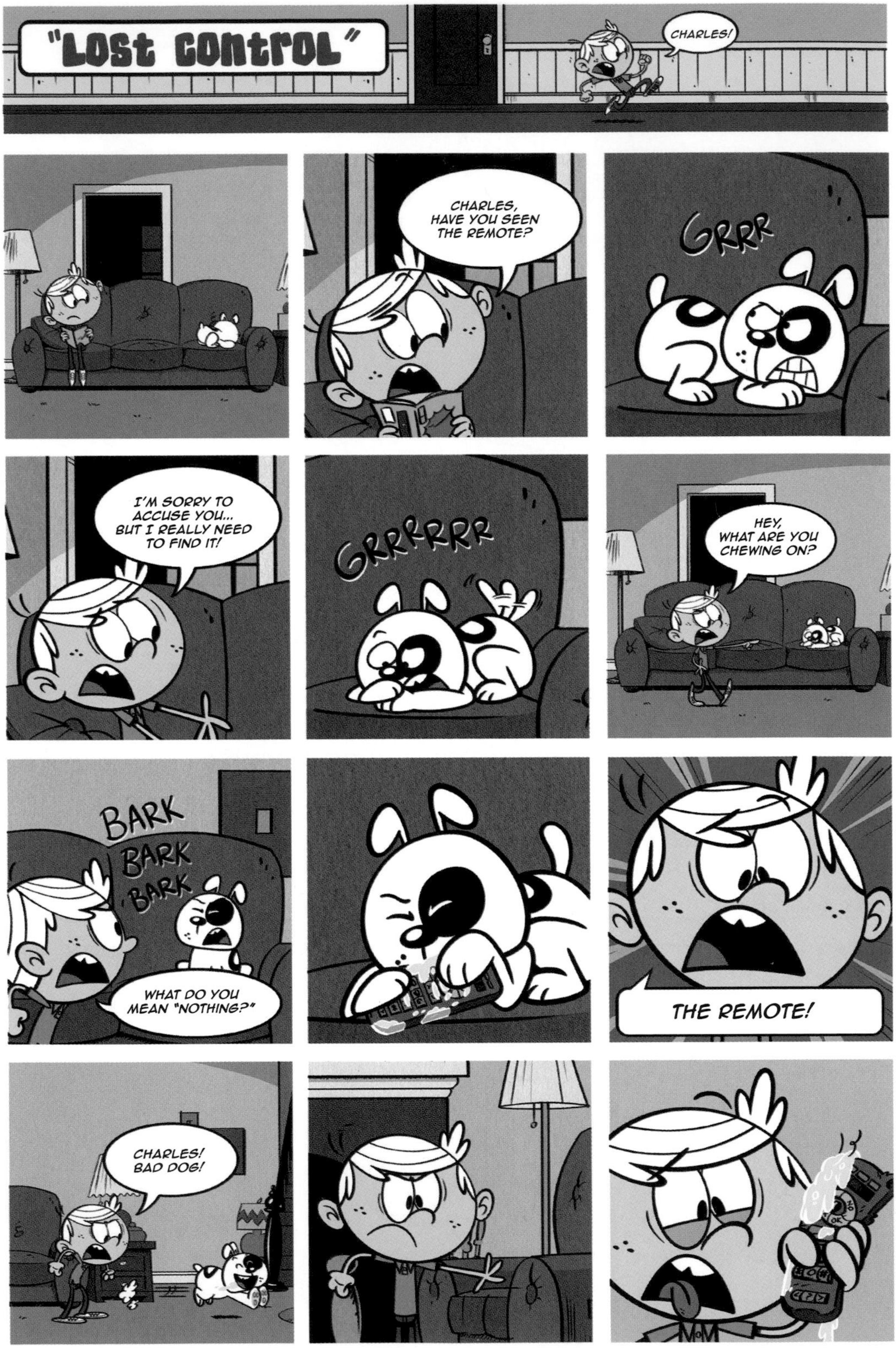
"LOST CONTROL"
CHARLES!
CHARLES, HAVE YOU SEEN THE REMOTE?
GRRR
I'M SORRY TO ACCUSE YOU... BUT I REALLY NEED TO FIND IT!
GRRRRRR
HEY, WHAT ARE YOU CHEWING ON?
BARK
BARK
BARK
WHAT DO YOU MEAN "NOTHING?"
THE REMOTE!
CHARLES! BAD DOG!

OH, NO! YOU'VE HIT A DEAD END. TO TRY AGAIN, GO TALK TO LORI ON PAGE 7.

"THE SPOT"

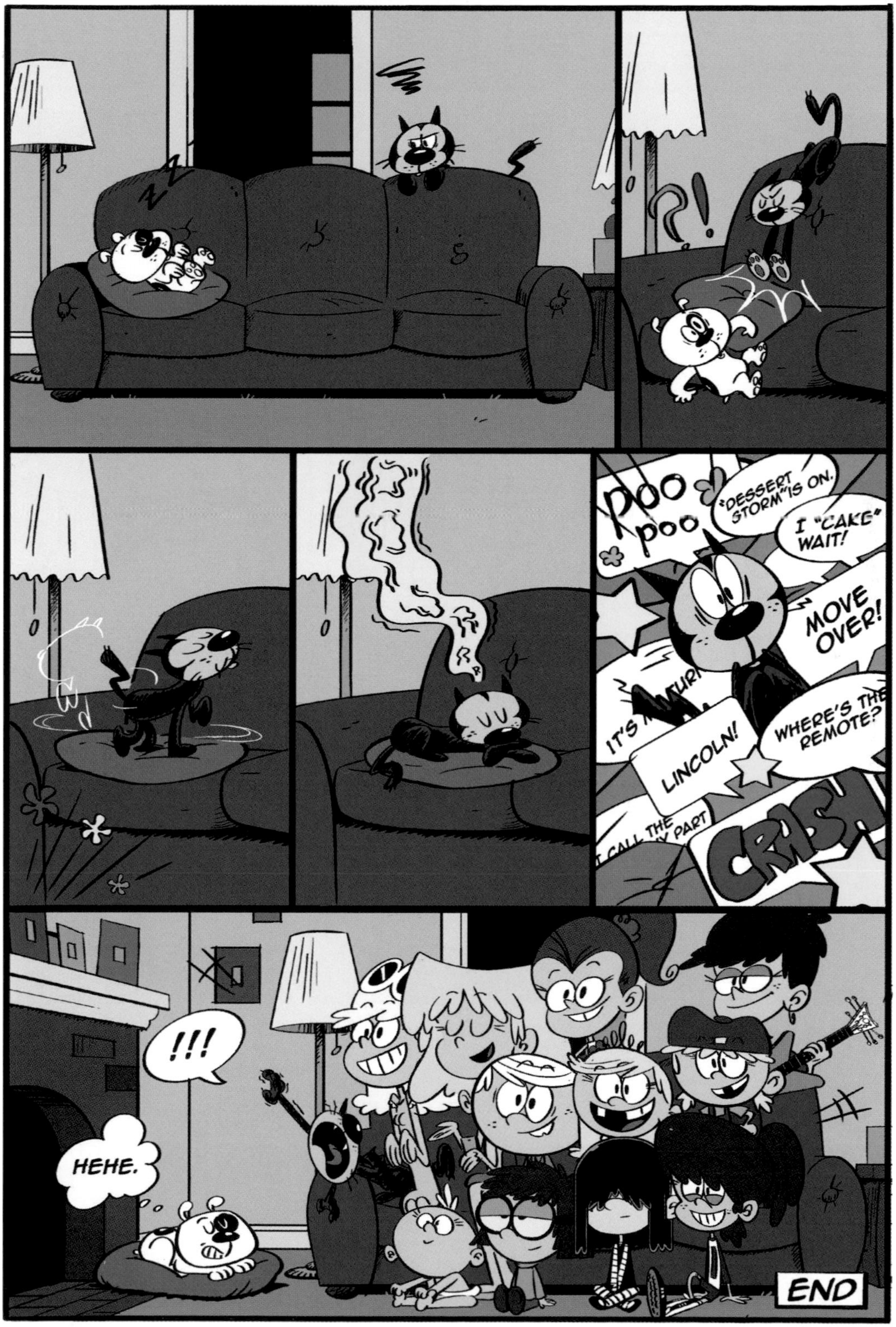

?!
POO
poo
"DESSERT STORM" IS ON.
I "CAKE" WAIT!
MOVE OVER!
WHERE'S THE REMOTE?
LINCOLN!
!!!
HEHE.
END

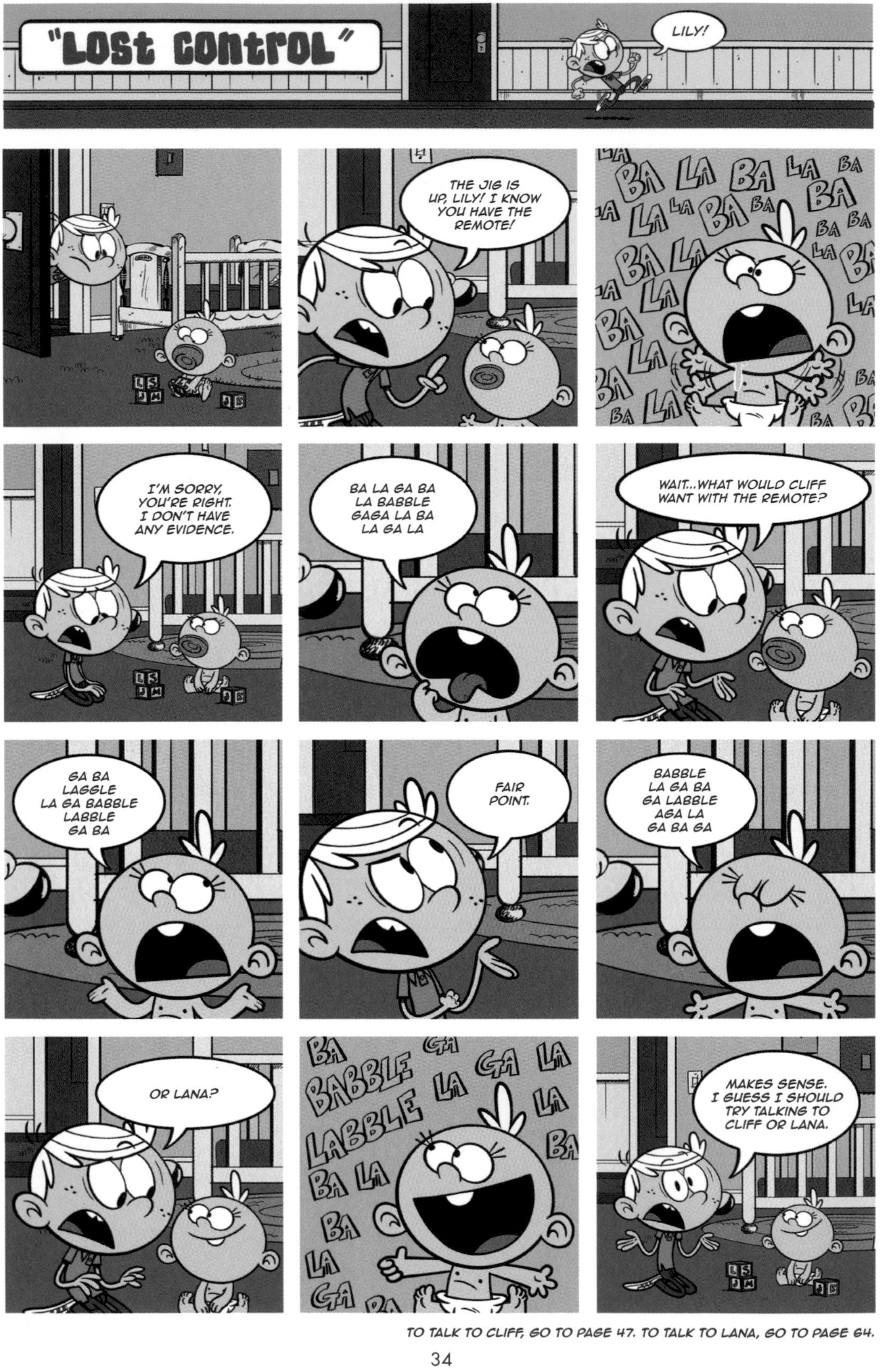
"Lost Control"
LILY!
THE JIG IS UP, LILY! I KNOW YOU HAVE THE REMOTE!
BA LA BA LA BA
LA LA BA BA BA
BA BA BA LA BA
BA LA BA LA
I'M SORRY, YOU'RE RIGHT. I DON'T HAVE ANY EVIDENCE.
BA LA GA BA LA BABBLE GAGA LA BA LA GA LA
WAIT...WHAT WOULD CLIFF WANT WITH THE REMOTE?
GA BA LAGGLE LA GA BABBLE LABBLE GA BA
FAIR POINT.
BABBLE LA GA BA GA LABBLE AGA LA GA BA GA
OR LANA?
BA BABBLE GA LA GA LA LABBLE LA LA BA
BA LA BA LA GA BA
MAKES SENSE. I GUESS I SHOULD TRY TALKING TO CLIFF OR LANA.

TO TALK TO CLIFF, GO TO PAGE 47. TO TALK TO LANA, GO TO PAGE 64.

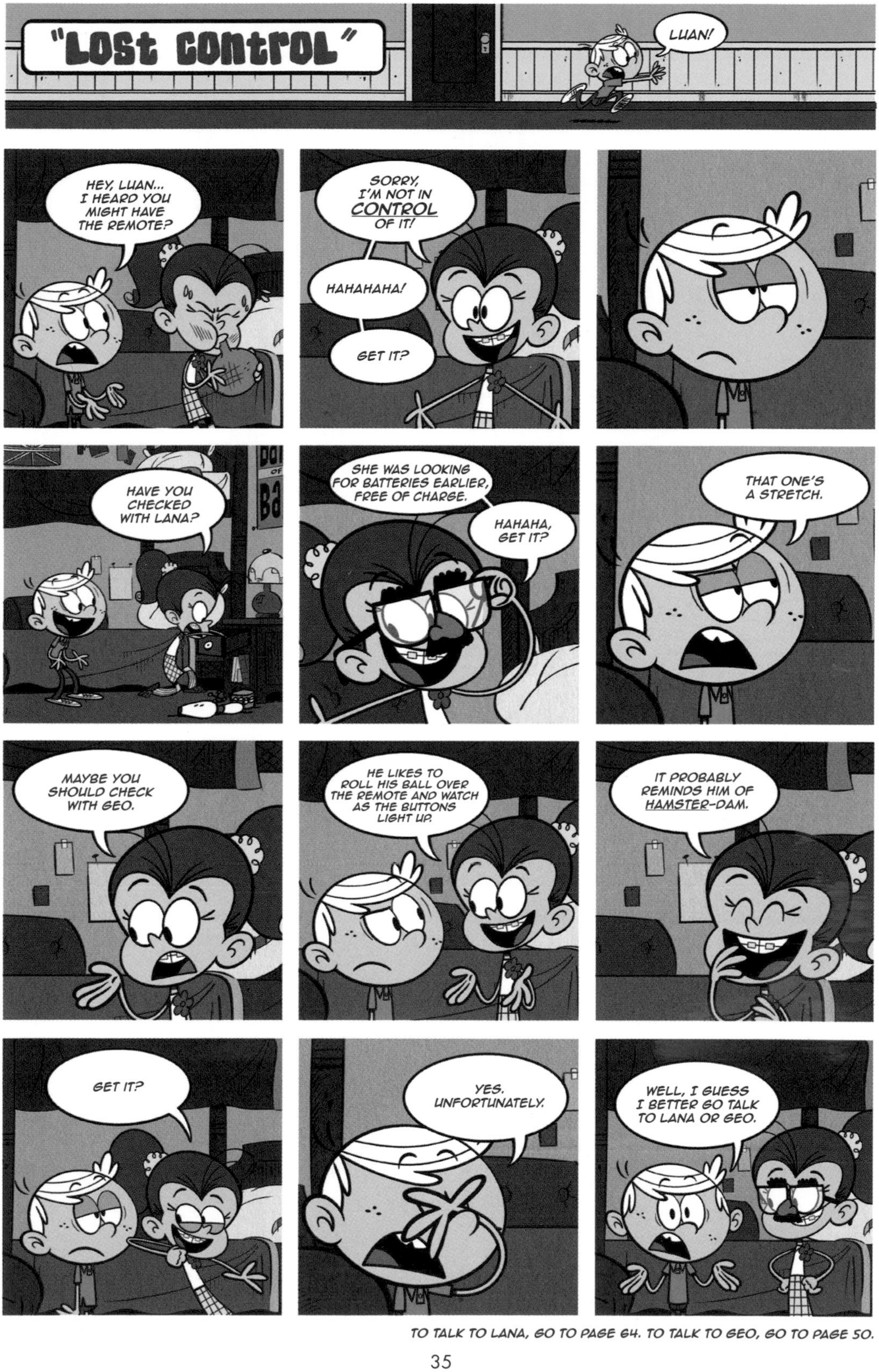
"LOST CONTROL"
LUAN!
HEY, LUAN... I HEARD YOU MIGHT HAVE THE REMOTE?
SORRY, I'M NOT IN CONTROL OF IT!
HAHAHAHA!
GET IT?
HAVE YOU CHECKED WITH LANA?
SHE WAS LOOKING FOR BATTERIES EARLIER, FREE OF CHARGE.
HAHAHA, GET IT?
THAT ONE'S A STRETCH.
MAYBE YOU SHOULD CHECK WITH GEO.
HE LIKES TO ROLL HIS BALL OVER THE REMOTE AND WATCH AS THE BUTTONS LIGHT UP.
IT PROBABLY REMINDS HIM OF HAMSTER-DAM.
GET IT?
YES. UNFORTUNATELY.
WELL, I GUESS I BETTER GO TALK TO LANA OR GEO.

TO TALK TO LANA, GO TO PAGE 64. TO TALK TO GEO, GO TO PAGE 50.

“NO SPOILERS”

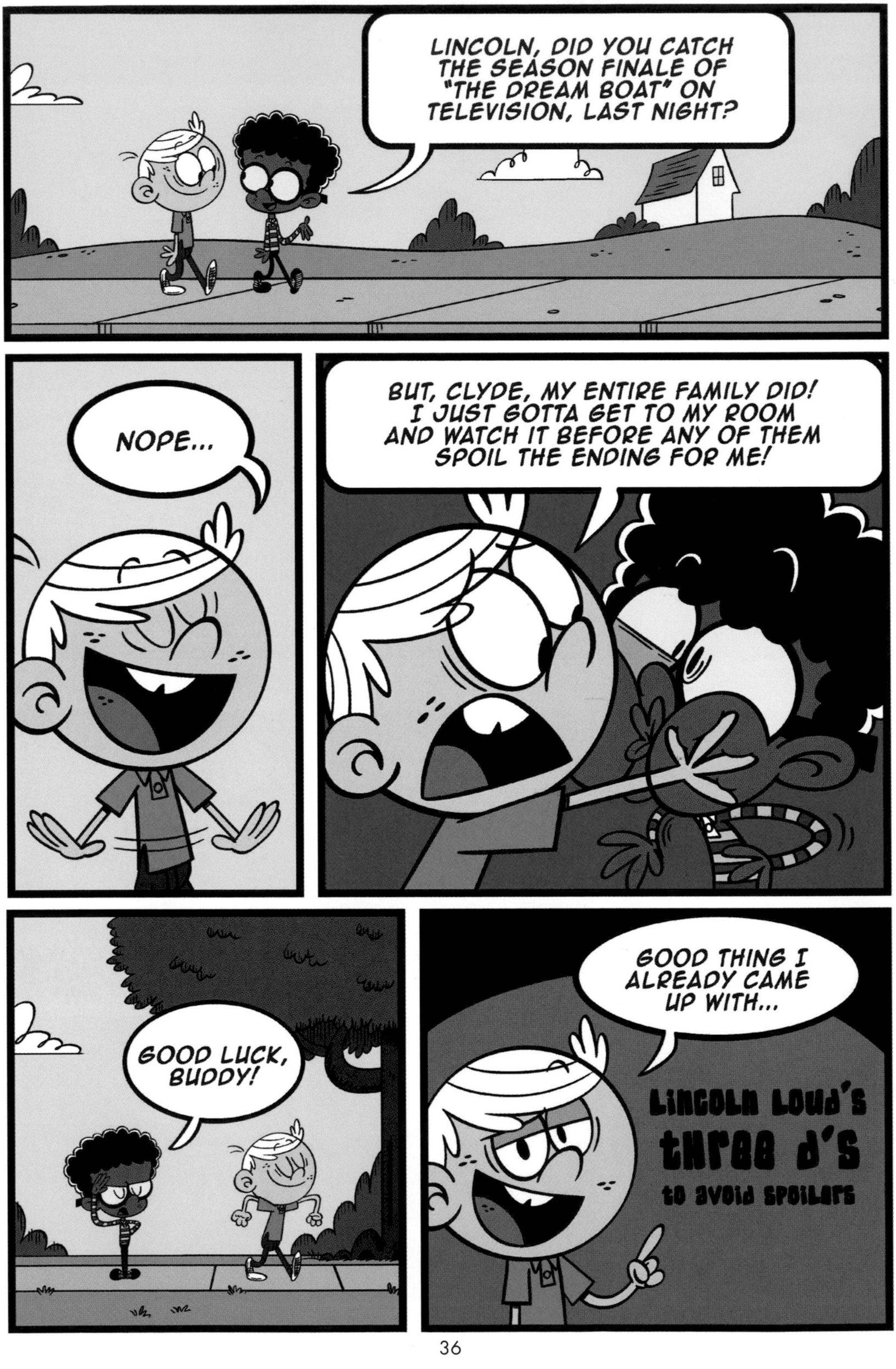

LINCOLN, DID YOU CATCH THE SEASON FINALE OF "THE DREAM BOAT" ON TELEVISION, LAST NIGHT?
NOPE...
BUT, CLYDE, MY ENTIRE FAMILY DID! I JUST GOTTA GET TO MY ROOM AND WATCH IT BEFORE ANY OF THEM SPOIL THE ENDING FOR ME!
GOOD LUCK, BUDDY!
GOOD THING I ALREADY CAME UP WITH...
LINCOLN LOUD'S THREE D'S TO AVOID SPOILERS

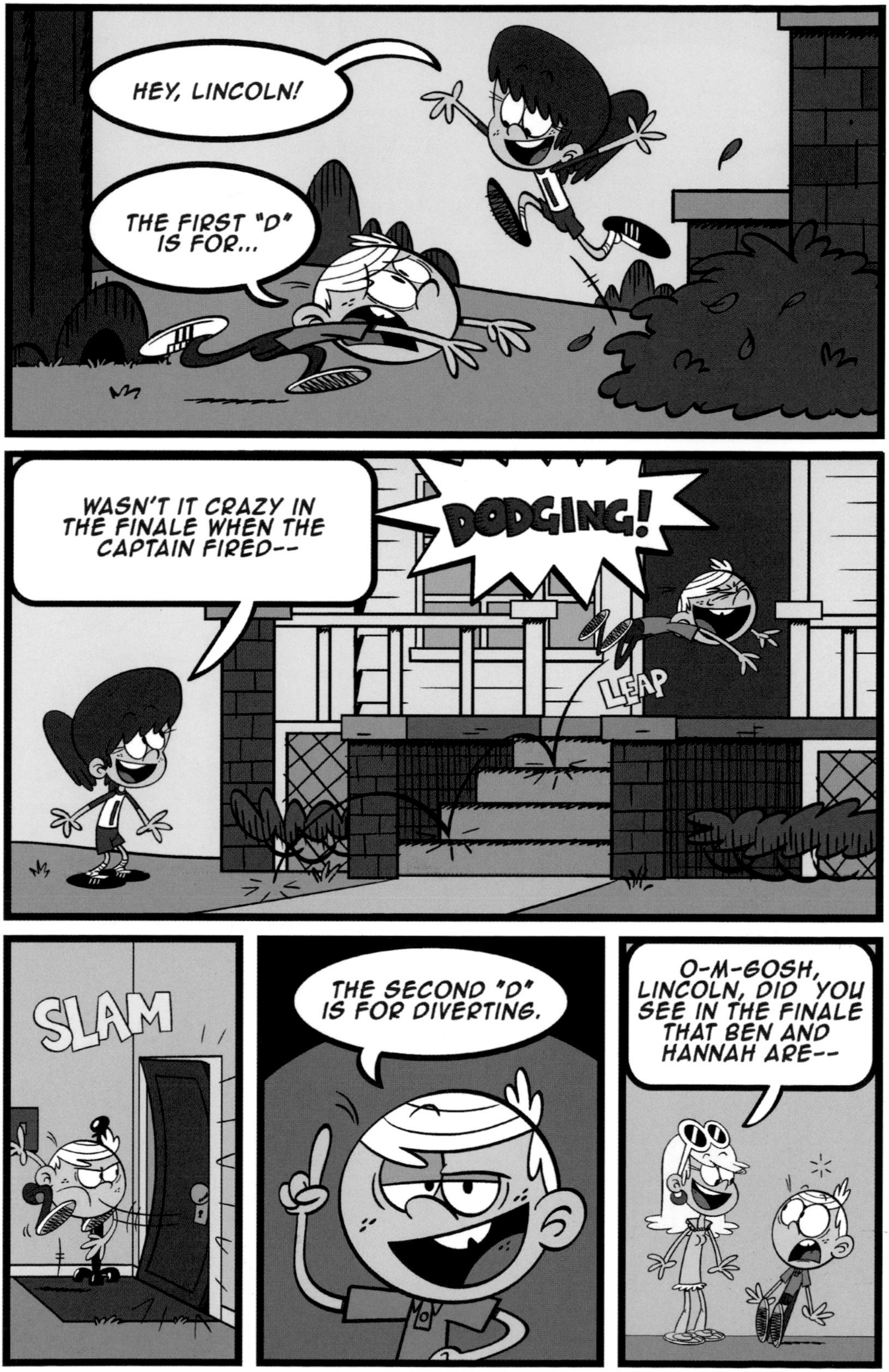
HEY, LINCOLN!
THE FIRST "D" IS FOR...
WASN'T IT CRAZY IN THE FINALE WHEN THE CAPTAIN FIRED--
DODGING!
LEAP
SLAM
THE SECOND "D" IS FOR DIVERTING.
O-M-GOSH, LINCOLN, DID YOU SEE IN THE FINALE THAT BEN AND HANNAH ARE--

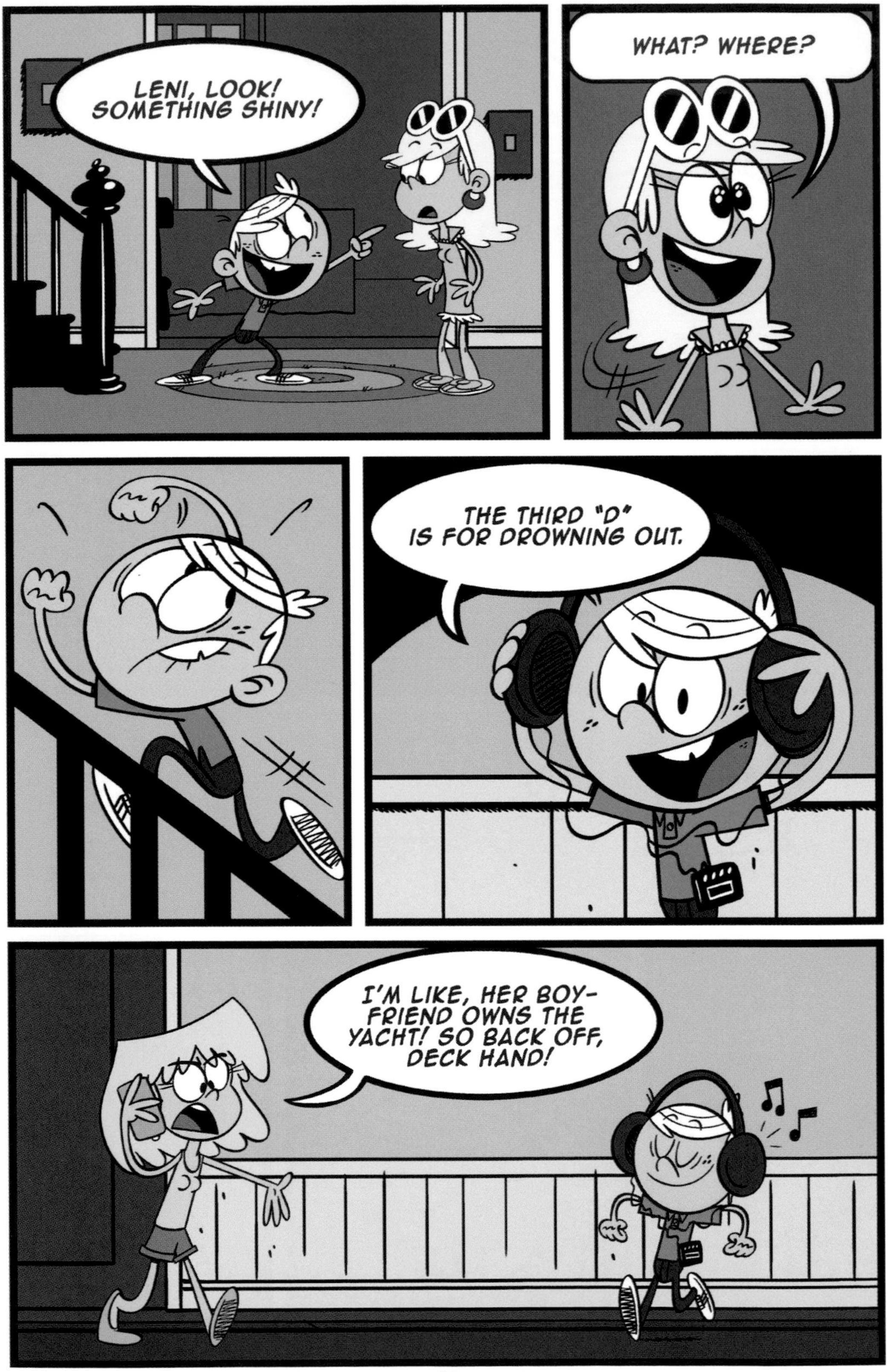
LENI, LOOK! SOMETHING SHINY!
WHAT? WHERE?
THE THIRD "D" IS FOR DROWNING OUT.
I'M LIKE, HER BOY-FRIEND OWNS THE YACHT! SO BACK OFF, DECK HAND!

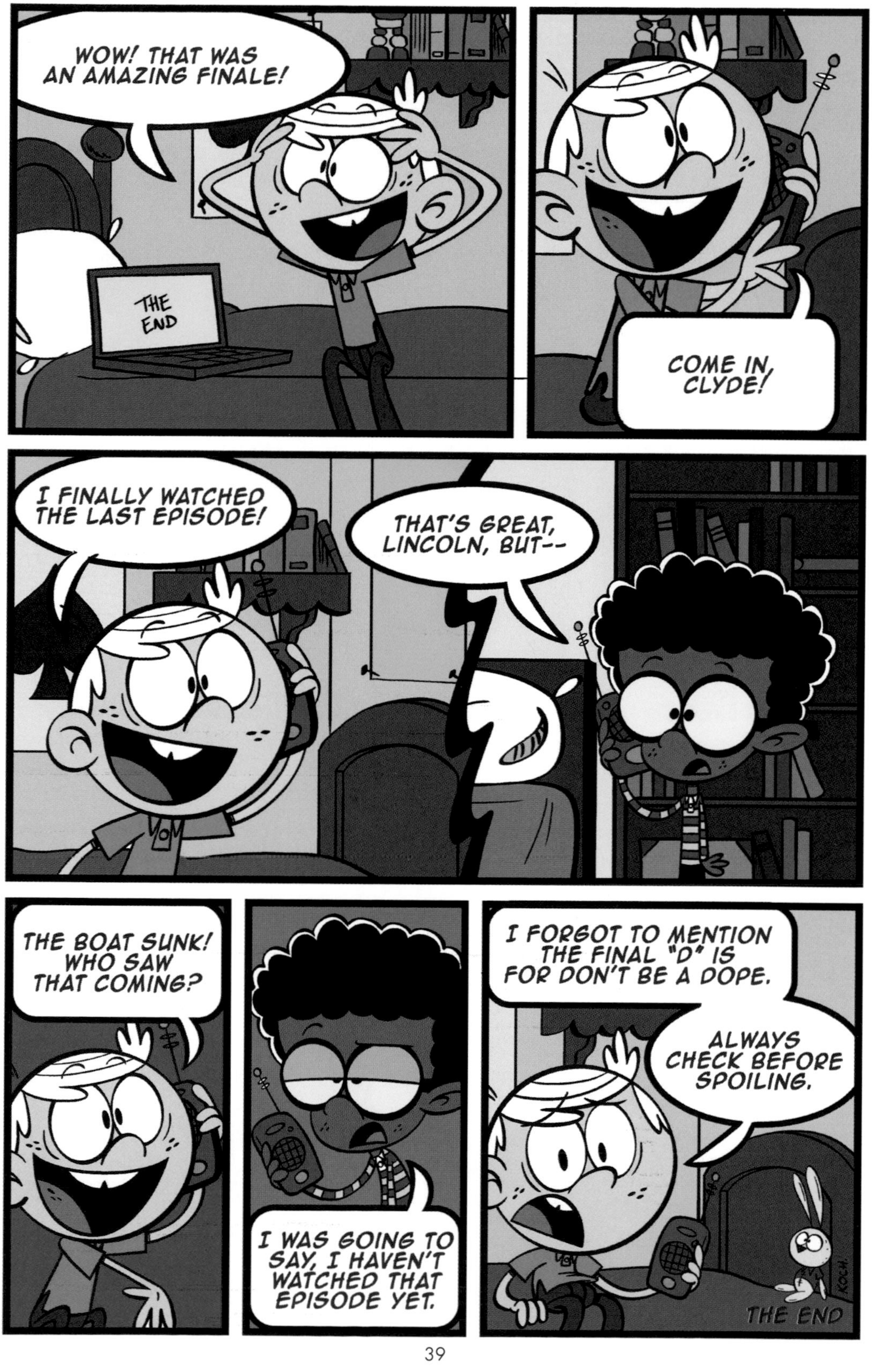
WOW! THAT WAS AN AMAZING FINALE!
THE END
COME IN, CLYDE!
I FINALLY WATCHED THE LAST EPISODE!
THAT'S GREAT, LINCOLN, BUT--
THE BOAT SUNK! WHO SAW THAT COMING?
I WAS GOING TO SAY, I HAVEN'T WATCHED THAT EPISODE YET.
I FORGOT TO MENTION THE FINAL "D" IS FOR DON'T BE A DOPE.
ALWAYS CHECK BEFORE SPOILING.
KOCH.
THE END

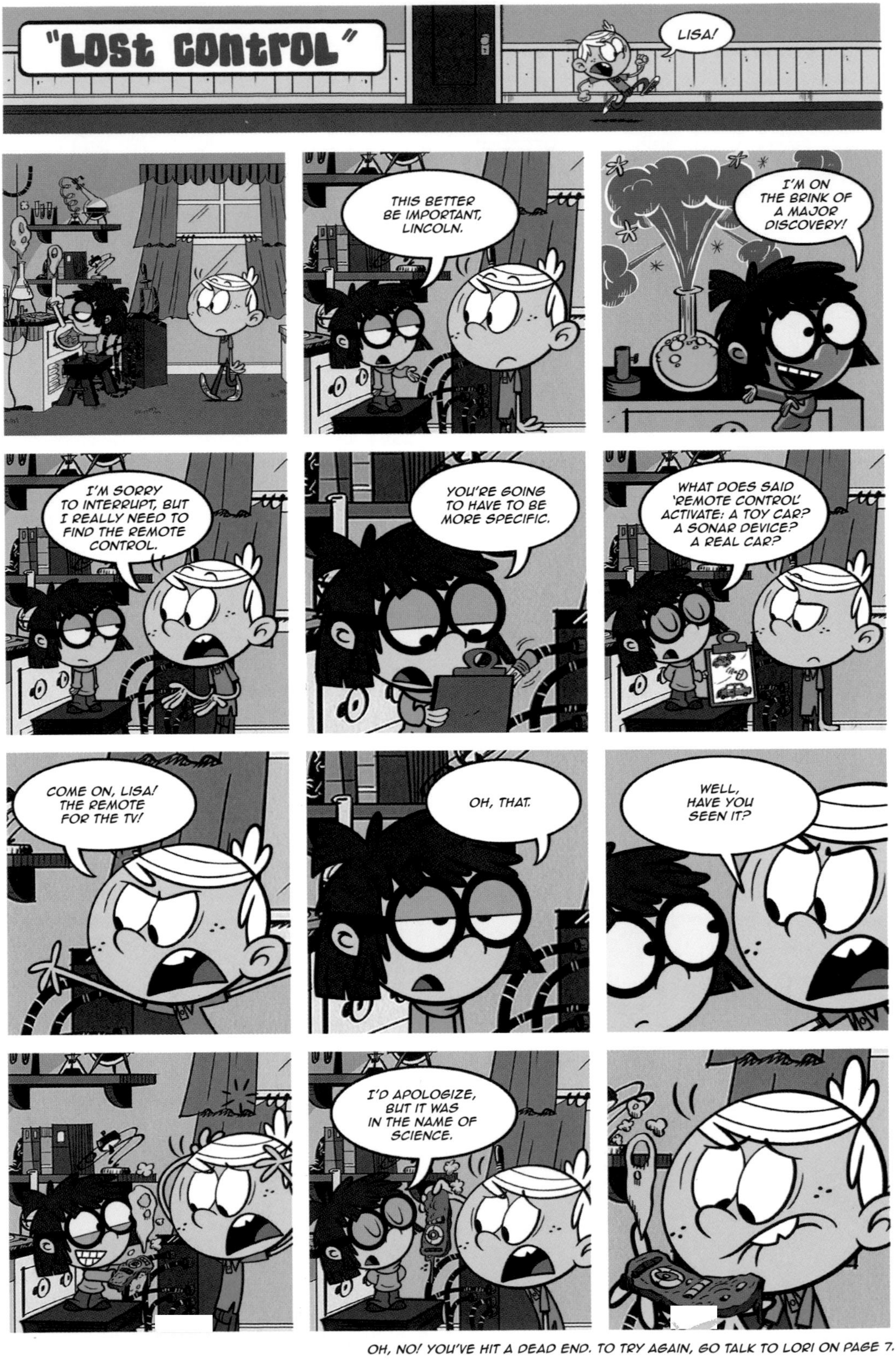

"LOST CONTROL"
LISA!
THIS BETTER BE IMPORTANT, LINCOLN.
I'M ON THE BRINK OF A MAJOR DISCOVERY!
I'M SORRY TO INTERRUPT, BUT I REALLY NEED TO FIND THE REMOTE CONTROL.
YOU'RE GOING TO HAVE TO BE MORE SPECIFIC.
WHAT DOES SAID 'REMOTE CONTROL' ACTIVATE: A TOY CAR? A SONAR DEVICE? A REAL CAR?
COME ON, LISA! THE REMOTE FOR THE TV!
OH, THAT.
WELL, HAVE YOU SEEN IT?
I'D APOLOGIZE, BUT IT WAS IN THE NAME OF SCIENCE.

OH, NO! YOU'VE HIT A DEAD END. TO TRY AGAIN, GO TALK TO LORI ON PAGE 7.

"THE CALL"

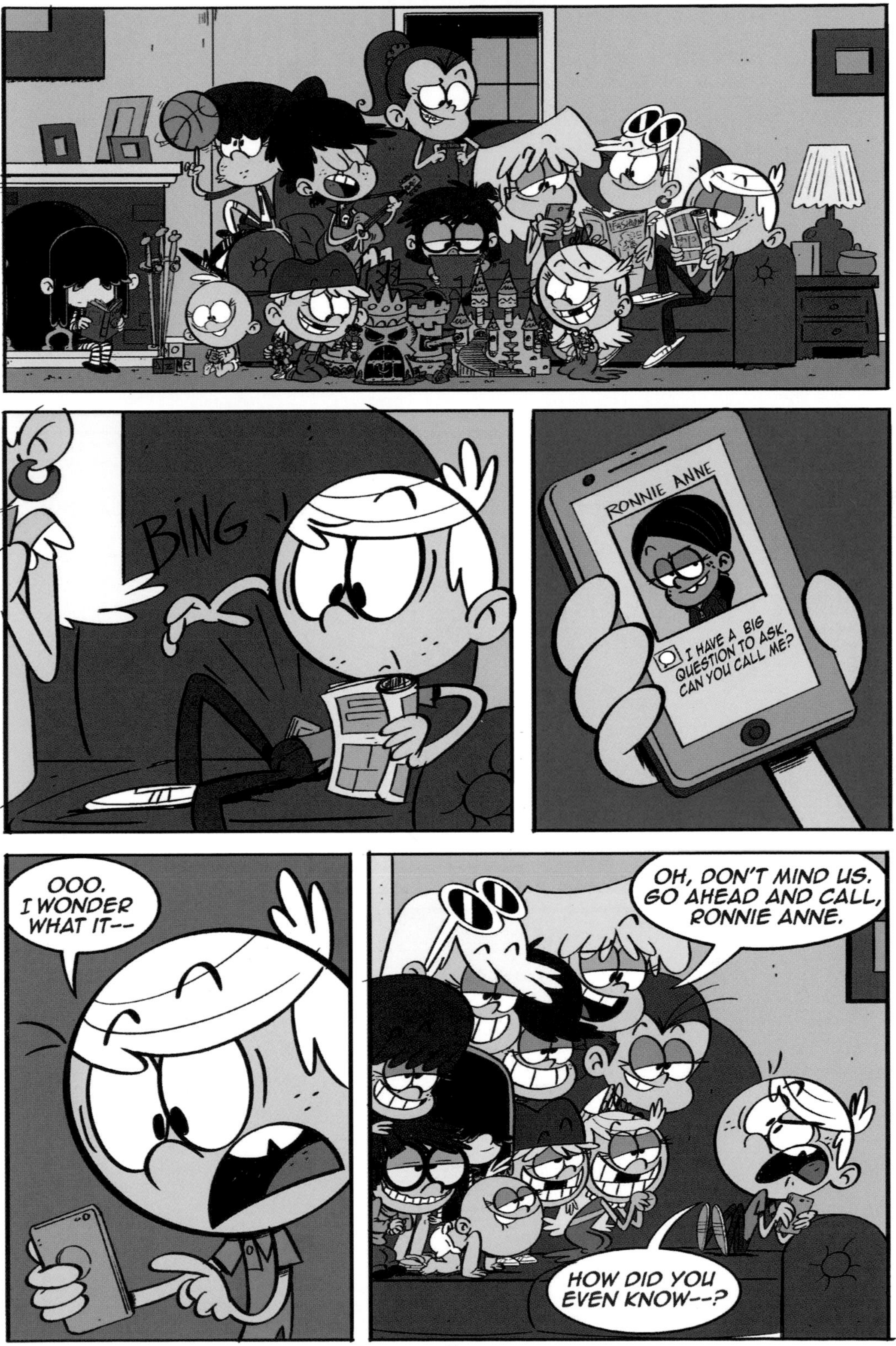
BING
RONNIE ANNE
I HAVE A BIG QUESTION TO ASK. CAN YOU CALL ME?
OOO. I WONDER WHAT IT--
OH, DON'T MIND US. GO AHEAD AND CALL, RONNIE ANNE.
HOW DID YOU EVEN KNOW--?

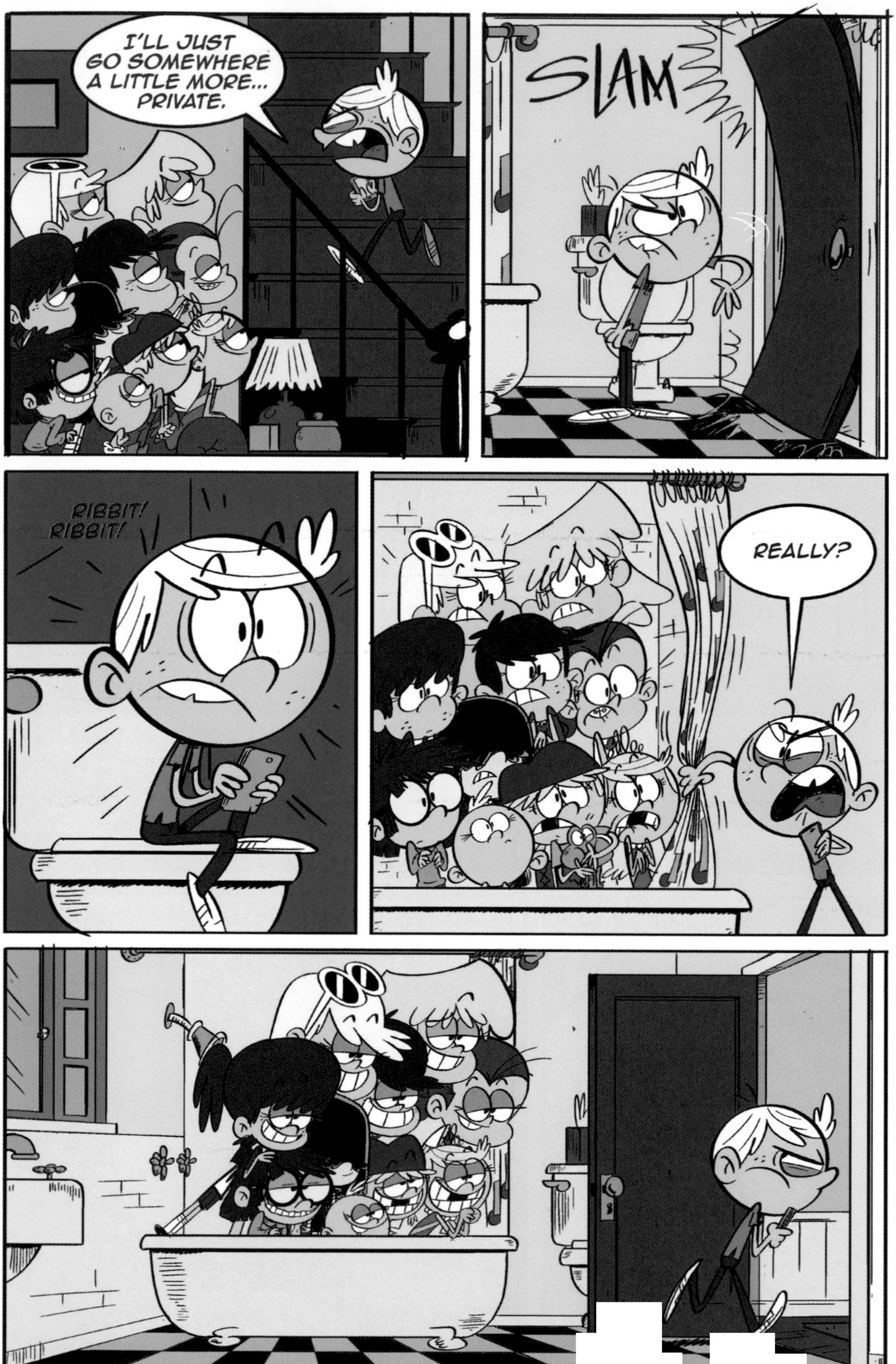
I'LL JUST GO SOMEWHERE A LITTLE MORE... PRIVATE.
SLAM
RIBBIT! RIBBIT!
REALLY?

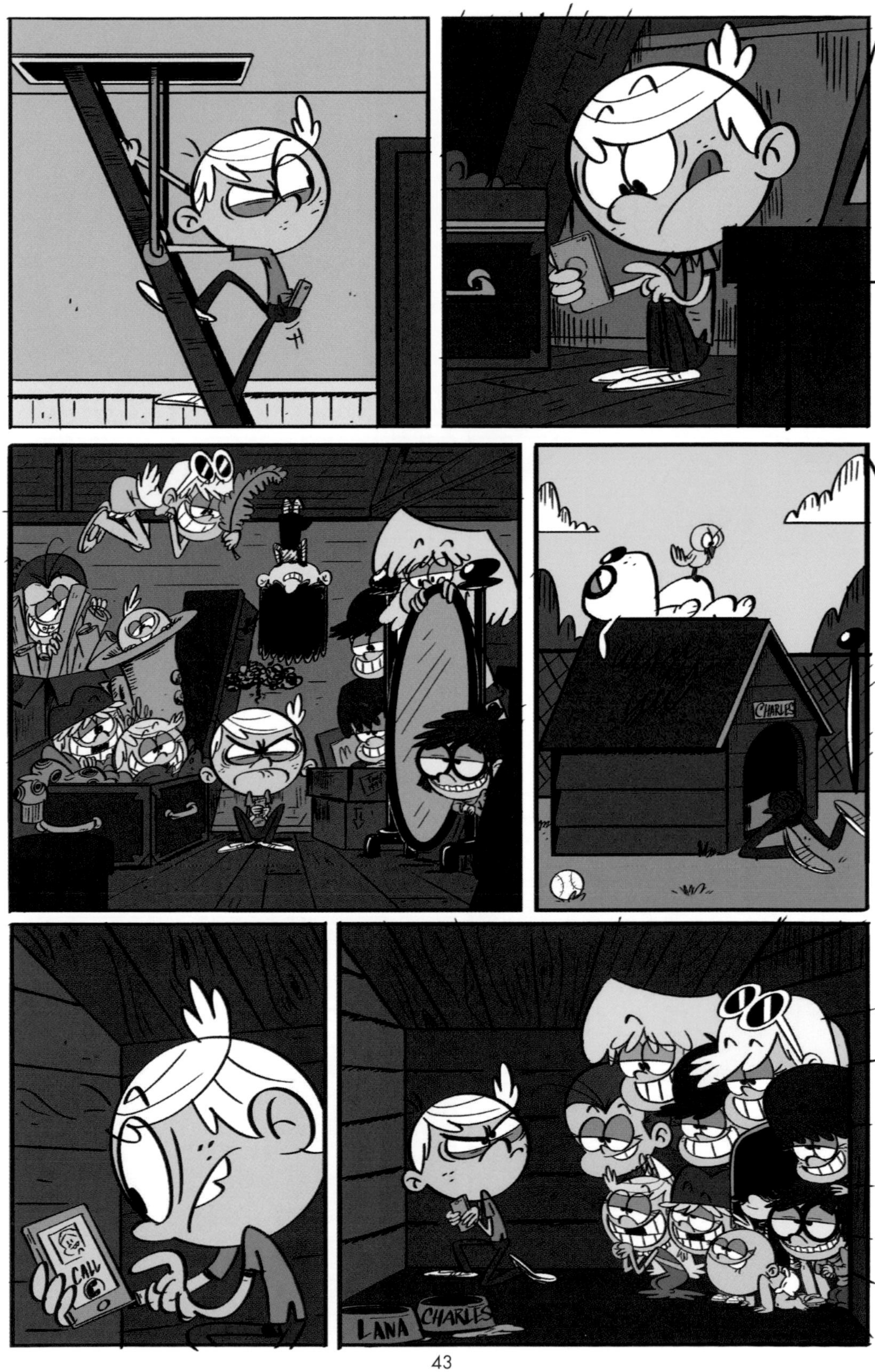
CHARLES
CALL
LANA
CHARLES

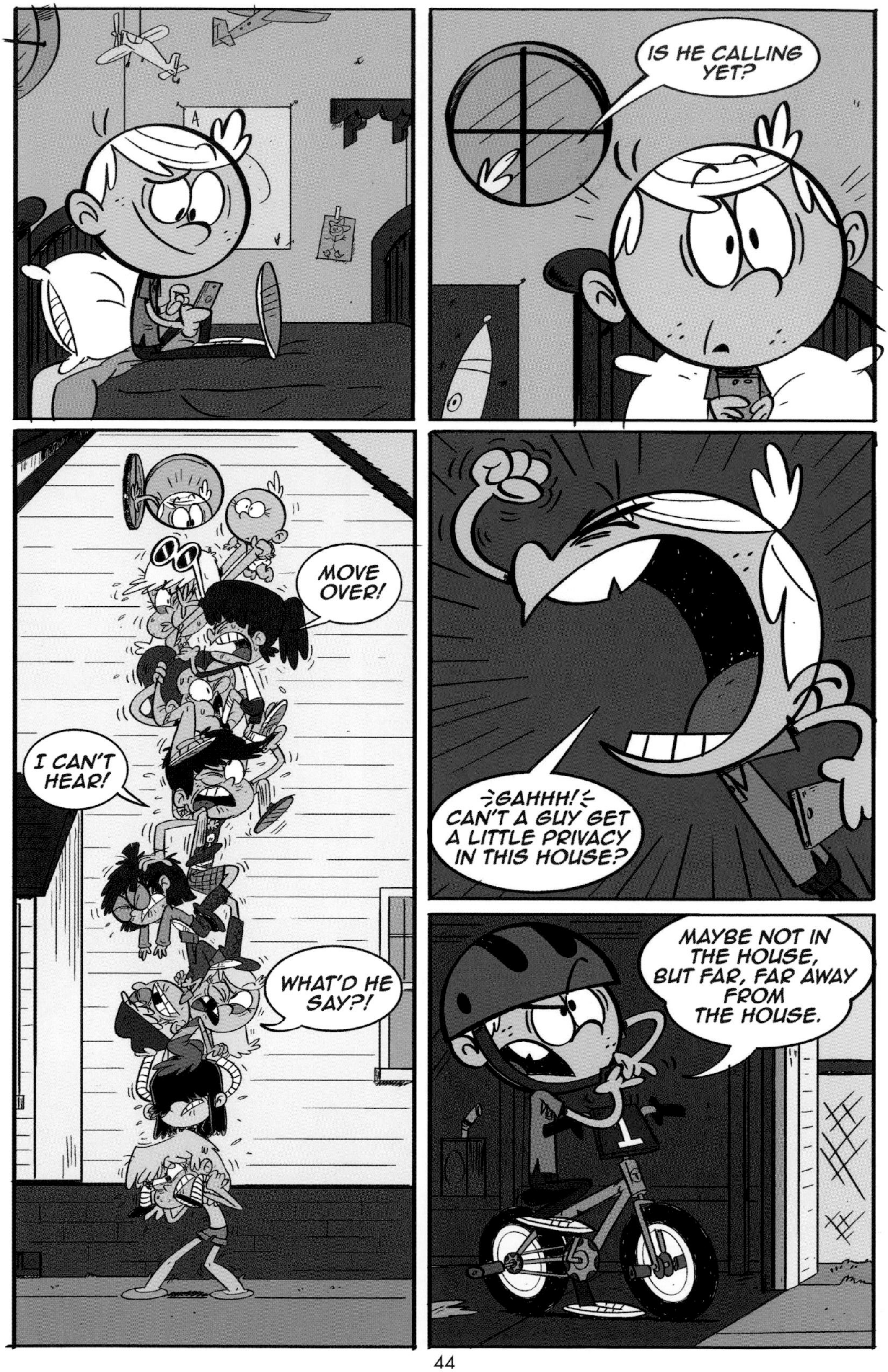
IS HE CALLING YET?
MOVE OVER!
I CAN'T HEAR!
WHAT'D HE SAY?!
GAHHH! CAN'T A GUY GET A LITTLE PRIVACY IN THIS HOUSE?
MAYBE NOT IN THE HOUSE, BUT FAR, FAR AWAY FROM THE HOUSE.

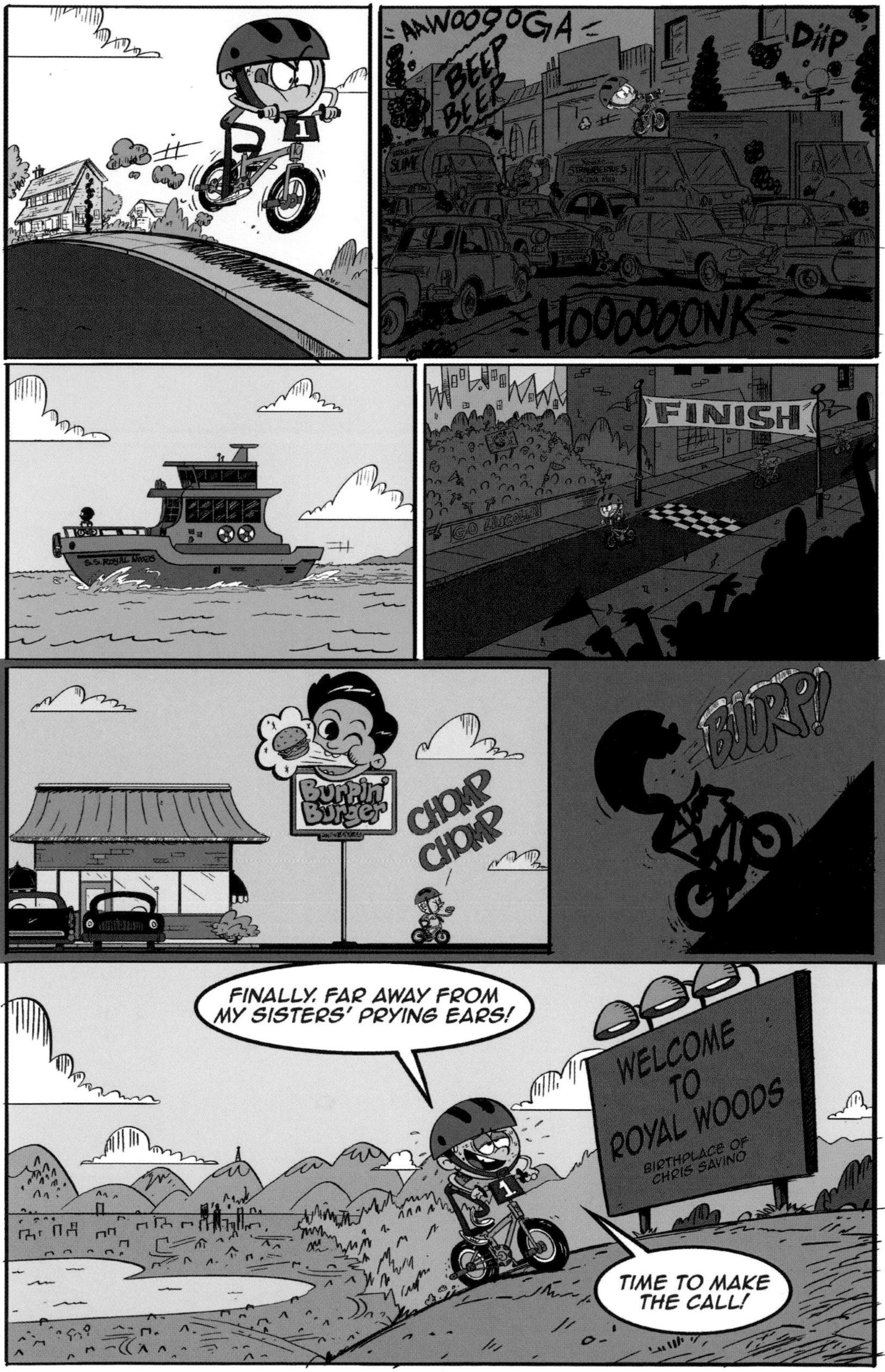
AAWOOGOGA
BEEP BEEP
DIIP
HOOOOOONK
S.S. ROYAL WOODS
FINISH
GO LINCOLN!
Burpin' Burger
CHOMP CHOMP
BUURP!
FINALLY. FAR AWAY FROM MY SISTERS' PRYING EARS!
WELCOME TO ROYAL WOODS
BIRTHPLACE OF CHRIS SAVINO
TIME TO MAKE THE CALL!

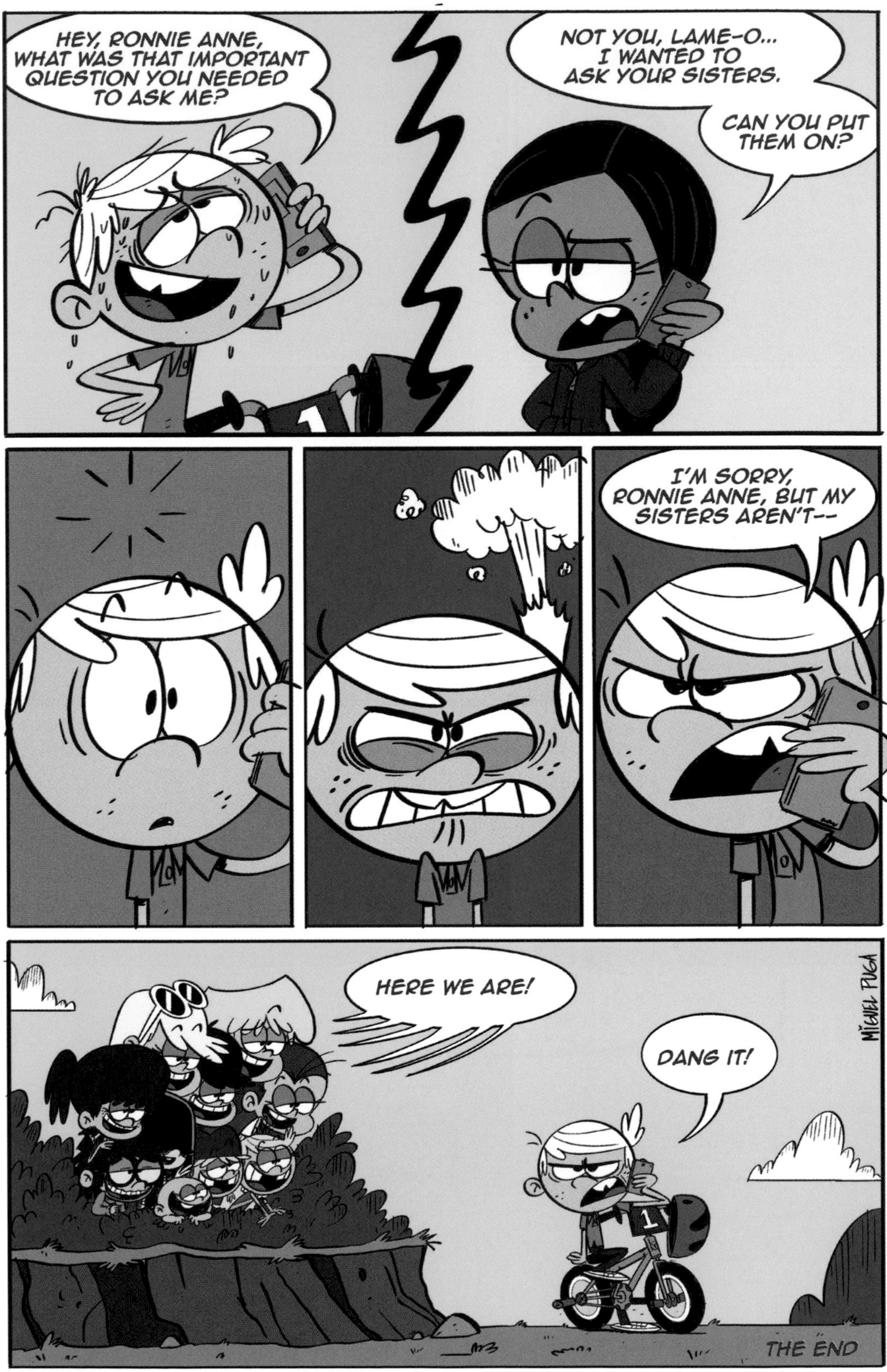
HEY, RONNIE ANNE, WHAT WAS THAT IMPORTANT QUESTION YOU NEEDED TO ASK ME?
NOT YOU, LAME-O... I WANTED TO ASK YOUR SISTERS.
CAN YOU PUT THEM ON?
I'M SORRY, RONNIE ANNE, BUT MY SISTERS AREN'T--
HERE WE ARE!
DANG IT!
MIGUEL PUGA
THE END

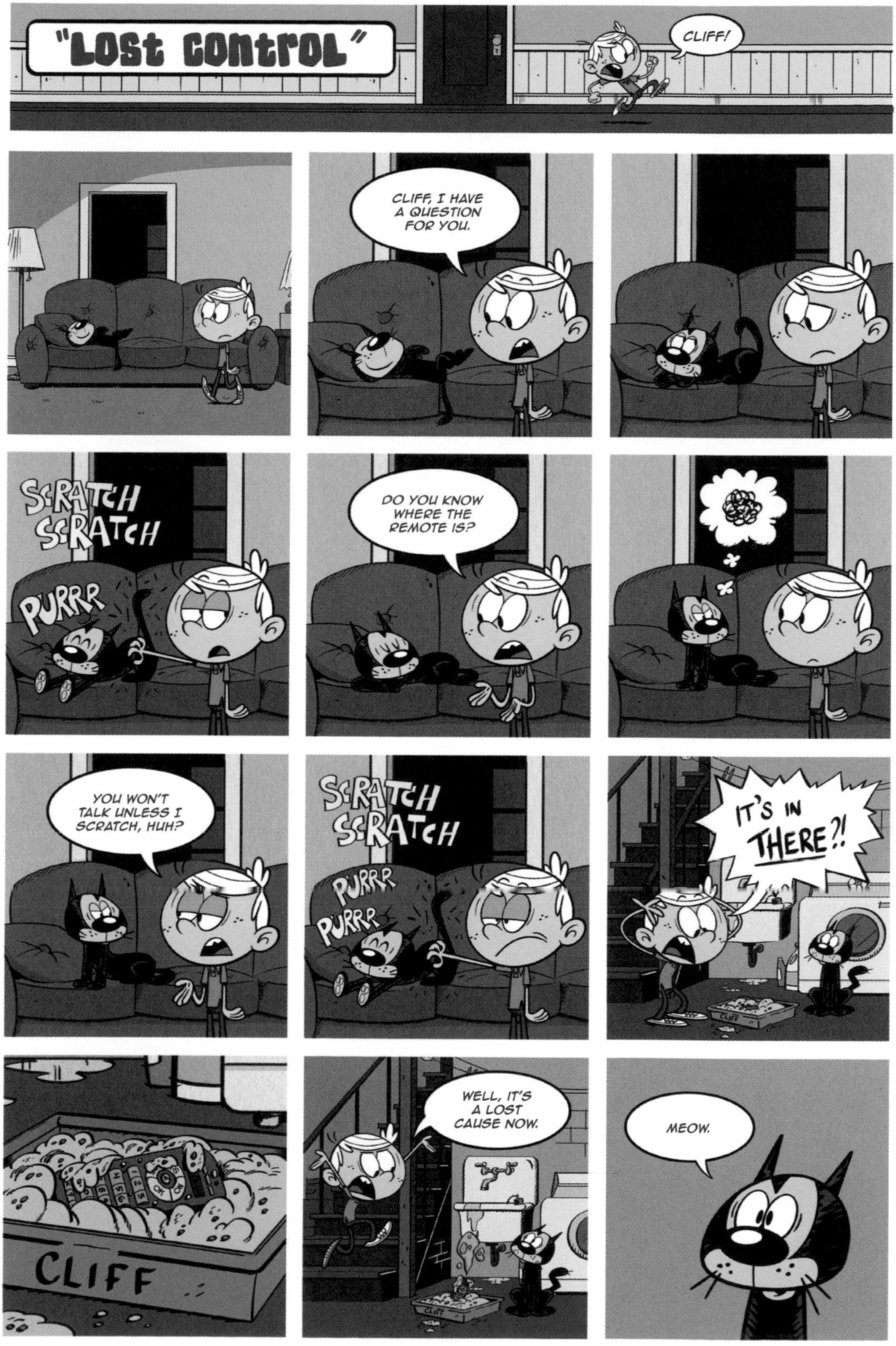
"LOST CONTROL"
CLIFF!
CLIFF, I HAVE A QUESTION FOR YOU.
SCRATCH SCRATCH
PURRR
DO YOU KNOW WHERE THE REMOTE IS?
YOU WON'T TALK UNLESS I SCRATCH, HUH?
SCRATCH SCRATCH
PURRR
PURRR
IT'S IN THERE?!
CLIFF
CLIFF
WELL, IT'S A LOST CAUSE NOW.
MEOW.

OH, NO! YOU'VE HIT A DEAD END. TO TRY AGAIN, GO TALK TO LORI ON PAGE 7.

“VERY SUPERSTITIOUS”

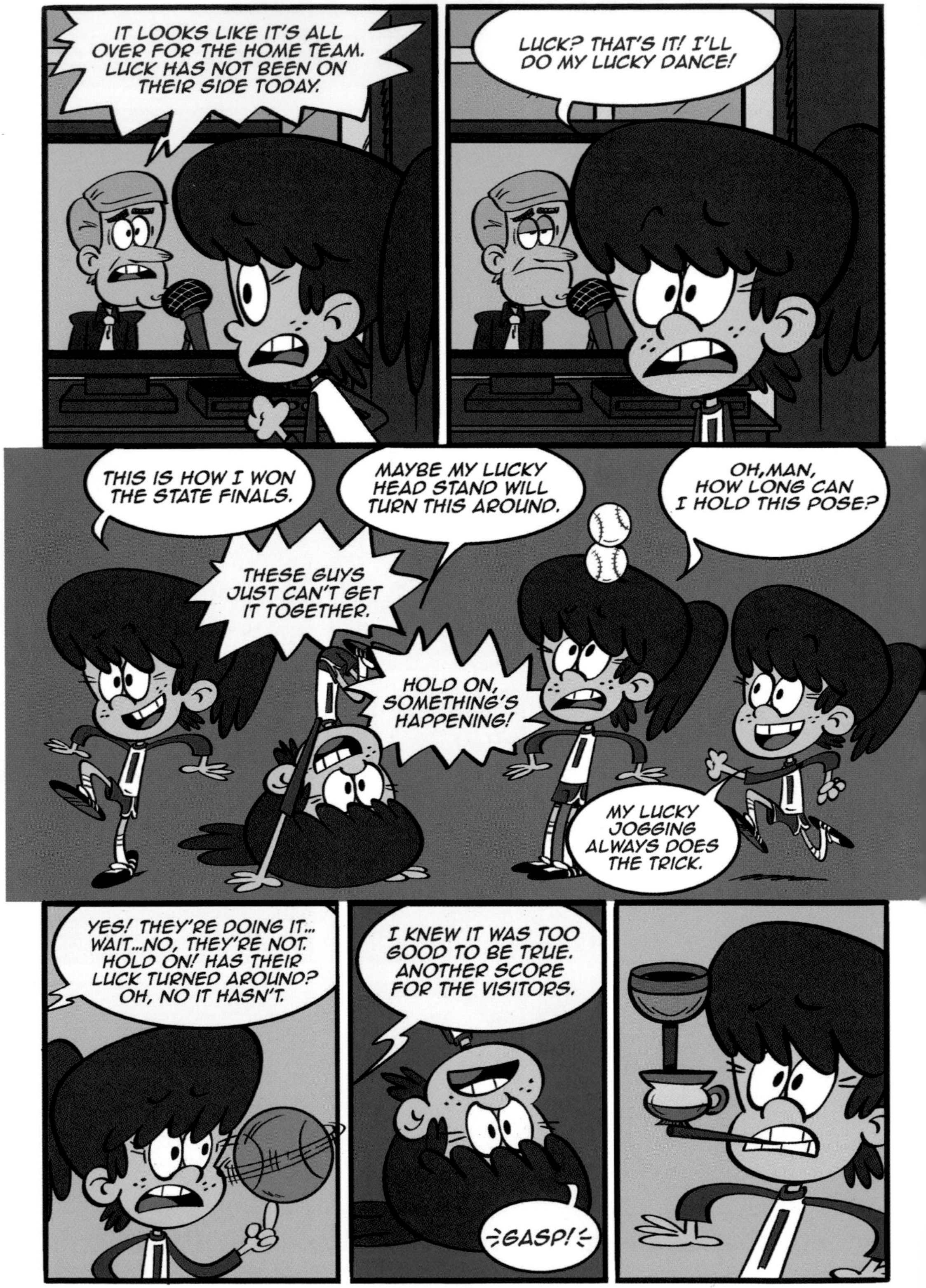

IT LOOKS LIKE IT'S ALL OVER FOR THE HOME TEAM. LUCK HAS NOT BEEN ON THEIR SIDE TODAY.
LUCK? THAT'S IT! I'LL DO MY LUCKY DANCE!
THIS IS HOW I WON THE STATE FINALS.
THESE GUYS JUST CAN'T GET IT TOGETHER.
MAYBE MY LUCKY HEAD STAND WILL TURN THIS AROUND.
HOLD ON, SOMETHING'S HAPPENING!
OH,MAN, HOW LONG CAN I HOLD THIS POSE?
MY LUCKY JOGGING ALWAYS DOES THE TRICK.
YES! THEY'RE DOING IT... WAIT...NO, THEY'RE NOT. HOLD ON! HAS THEIR LUCK TURNED AROUND? OH, NO IT HASN'T.
I KNEW IT WAS TOO GOOD TO BE TRUE. ANOTHER SCORE FOR THE VISITORS.
GASP!

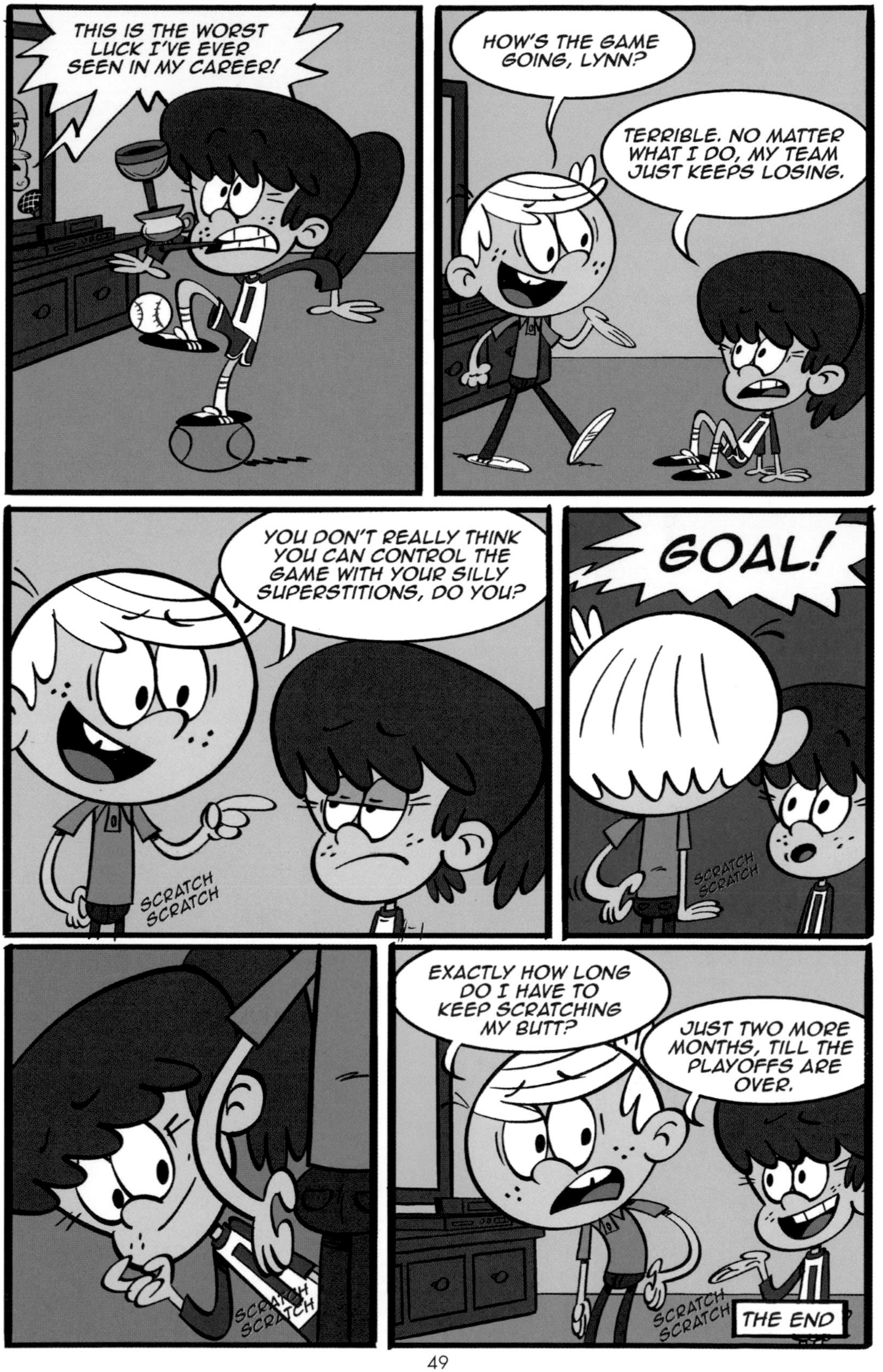
THIS IS THE WORST LUCK I'VE EVER SEEN IN MY CAREER!
HOW'S THE GAME GOING, LYNN?
TERRIBLE. NO MATTER WHAT I DO, MY TEAM JUST KEEPS LOSING.
YOU DON'T REALLY THINK YOU CAN CONTROL THE GAME WITH YOUR SILLY SUPERSTITIONS, DO YOU?
SCRATCH SCRATCH
GOAL!
SCRATCH SCRATCH
SCRATCH SCRATCH
EXACTLY HOW LONG DO I HAVE TO KEEP SCRATCHING MY BUTT?
JUST TWO MORE MONTHS, TILL THE PLAYOFFS ARE OVER.
SCRATCH SCRATCH
THE END

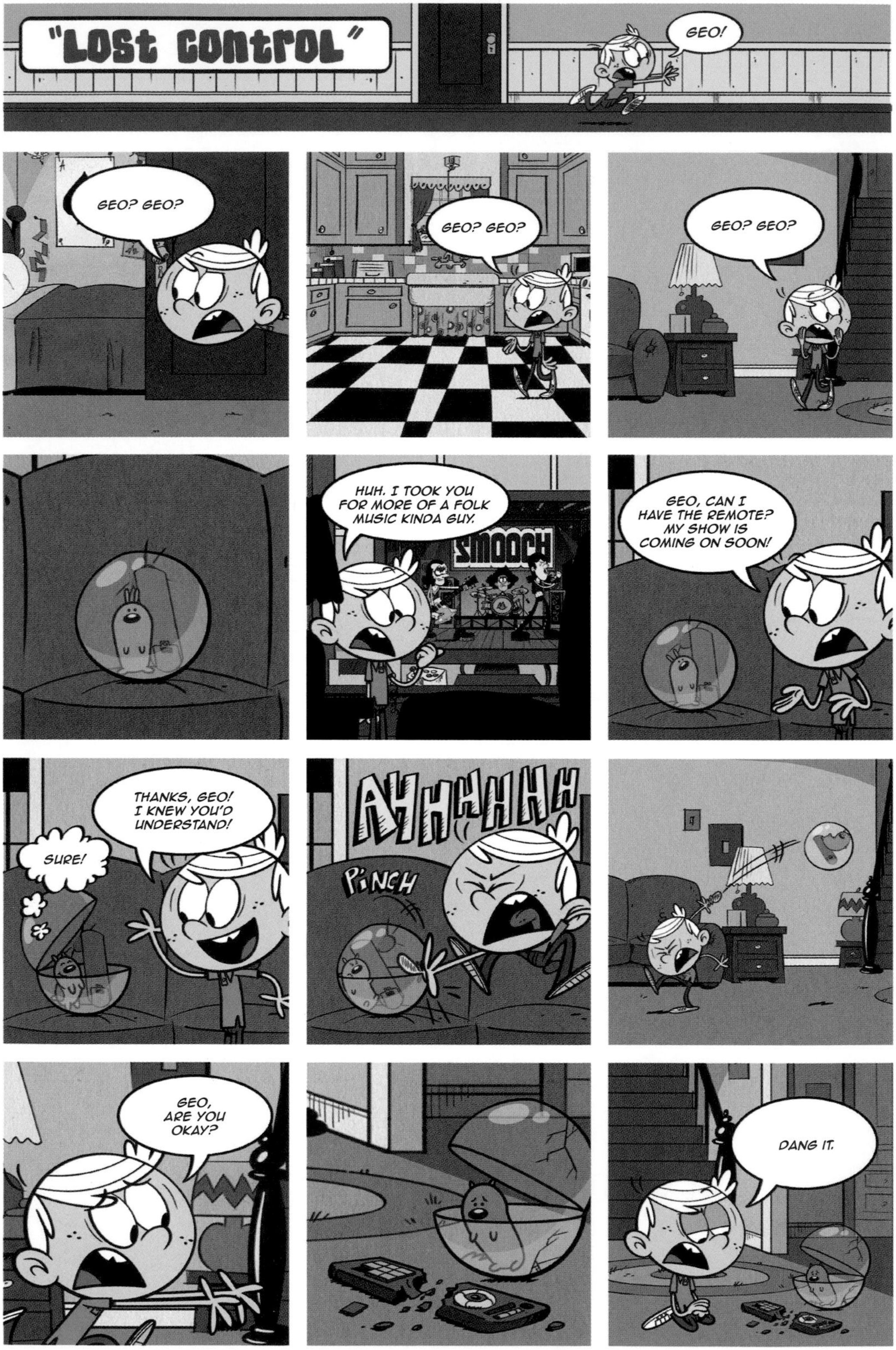
"LOST CONTROL"
GEO!
GEO? GEO?
GEO? GEO?
GEO? GEO?
HUH. I TOOK YOU FOR MORE OF A FOLK MUSIC KINDA GUY.
SMOOCH
GEO, CAN I HAVE THE REMOTE? MY SHOW IS COMING ON SOON!
THANKS, GEO! I KNEW YOU'D UNDERSTAND!
SURE!
AYHHHHHH
PINCH
GEO, ARE YOU OKAY?
DANG IT.

OH, NO! YOU'VE HIT A DEAD END. TO TRY AGAIN, GO TALK TO LORI ON PAGE 7.

“HERE COMES THE AIRPLANE”

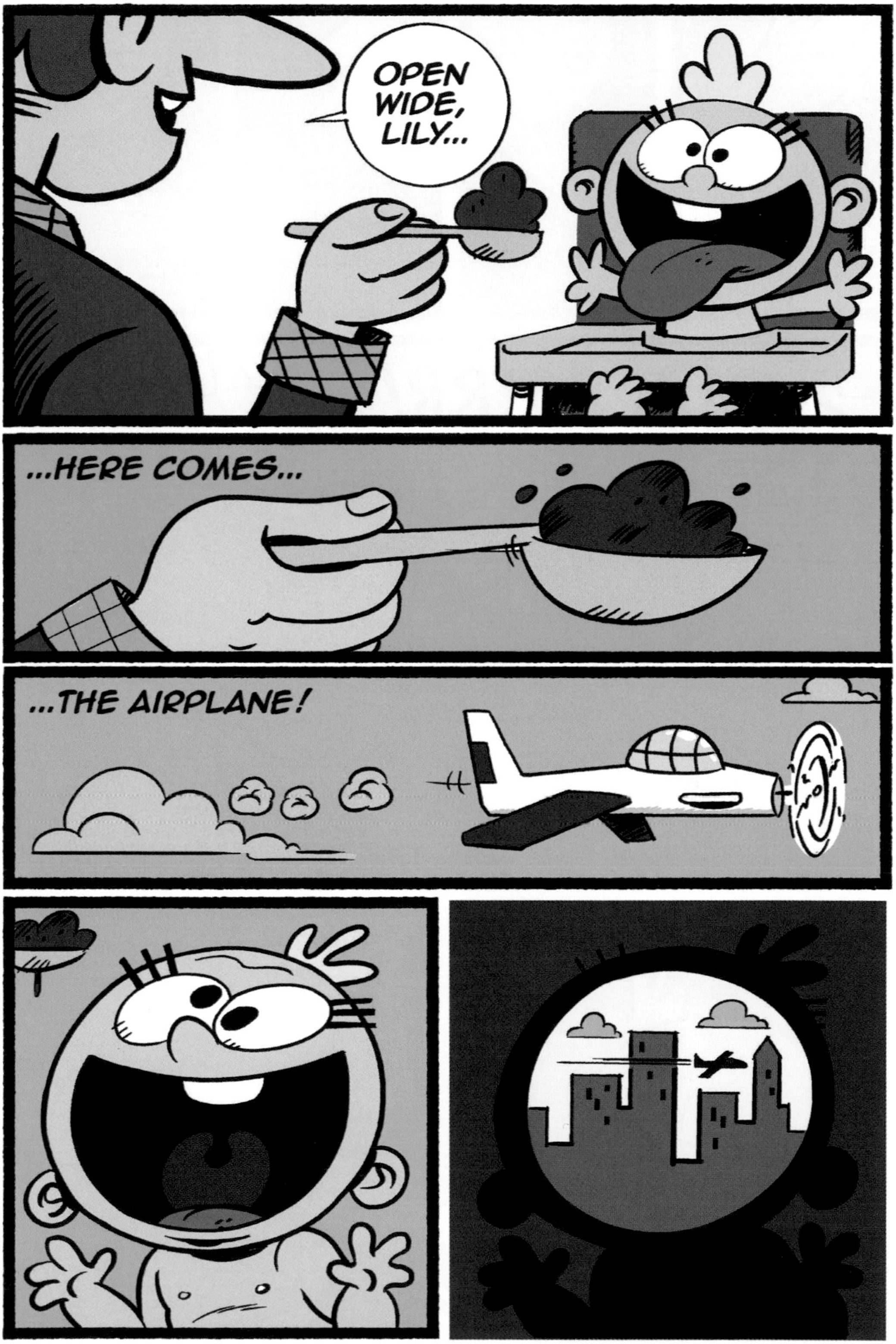
OPEN WIDE, LILY...
...HERE COMES...
...THE AIRPLANE!

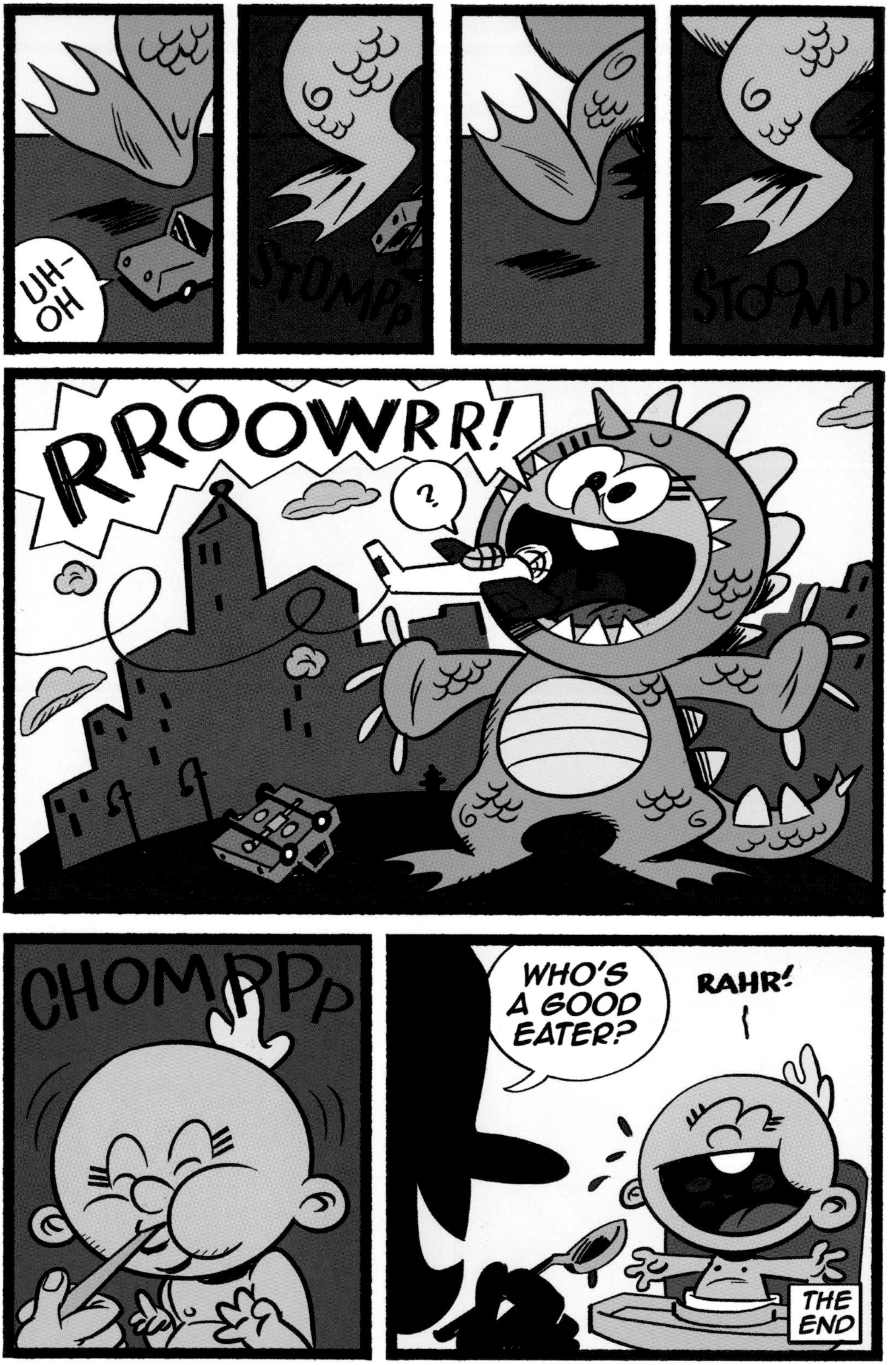
UH-OH
STOMPP
STOOOMP
RROOWRR!
?
CHOMPPP
WHO'S A GOOD EATER?
RAHR!
THE END

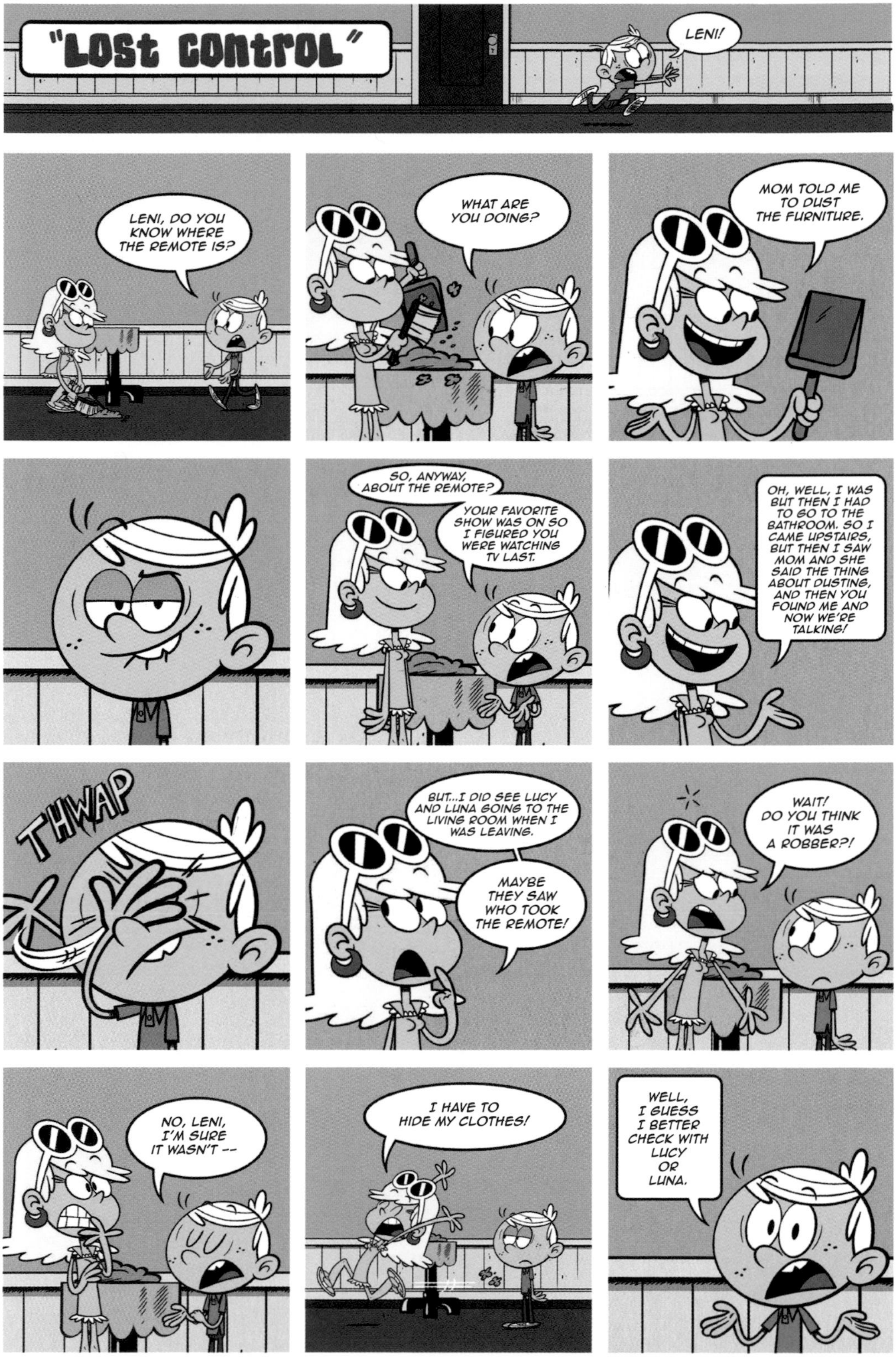
"LOST CONTROL"
LENI!
LENI, DO YOU KNOW WHERE THE REMOTE IS?
WHAT ARE YOU DOING?
MOM TOLD ME TO DUST THE FURNITURE.
SO, ANYWAY, ABOUT THE REMOTE?
YOUR FAVORITE SHOW WAS ON SO I FIGURED YOU WERE WATCHING TV LAST.
OH, WELL, I WAS BUT THEN I HAD TO GO TO THE BATHROOM. SO I CAME UPSTAIRS, BUT THEN I SAW MOM AND SHE SAID THE THING ABOUT DUSTING, AND THEN YOU FOUND ME AND NOW WE'RE TALKING!
THWAP
BUT...I DID SEE LUCY AND LUNA GOING TO THE LIVING ROOM WHEN I WAS LEAVING.
MAYBE THEY SAW WHO TOOK THE REMOTE!
WAIT! DO YOU THINK IT WAS A ROBBER?!
NO, LENI, I'M SURE IT WASN'T --
I HAVE TO HIDE MY CLOTHES!
WELL, I GUESS I BETTER CHECK WITH LUCY OR LUNA.

TO TALK TO LUCY, GO TO PAGE 25. TO TALK TO LUNA, GO TO PAGE 22.

"WALL WALKER"

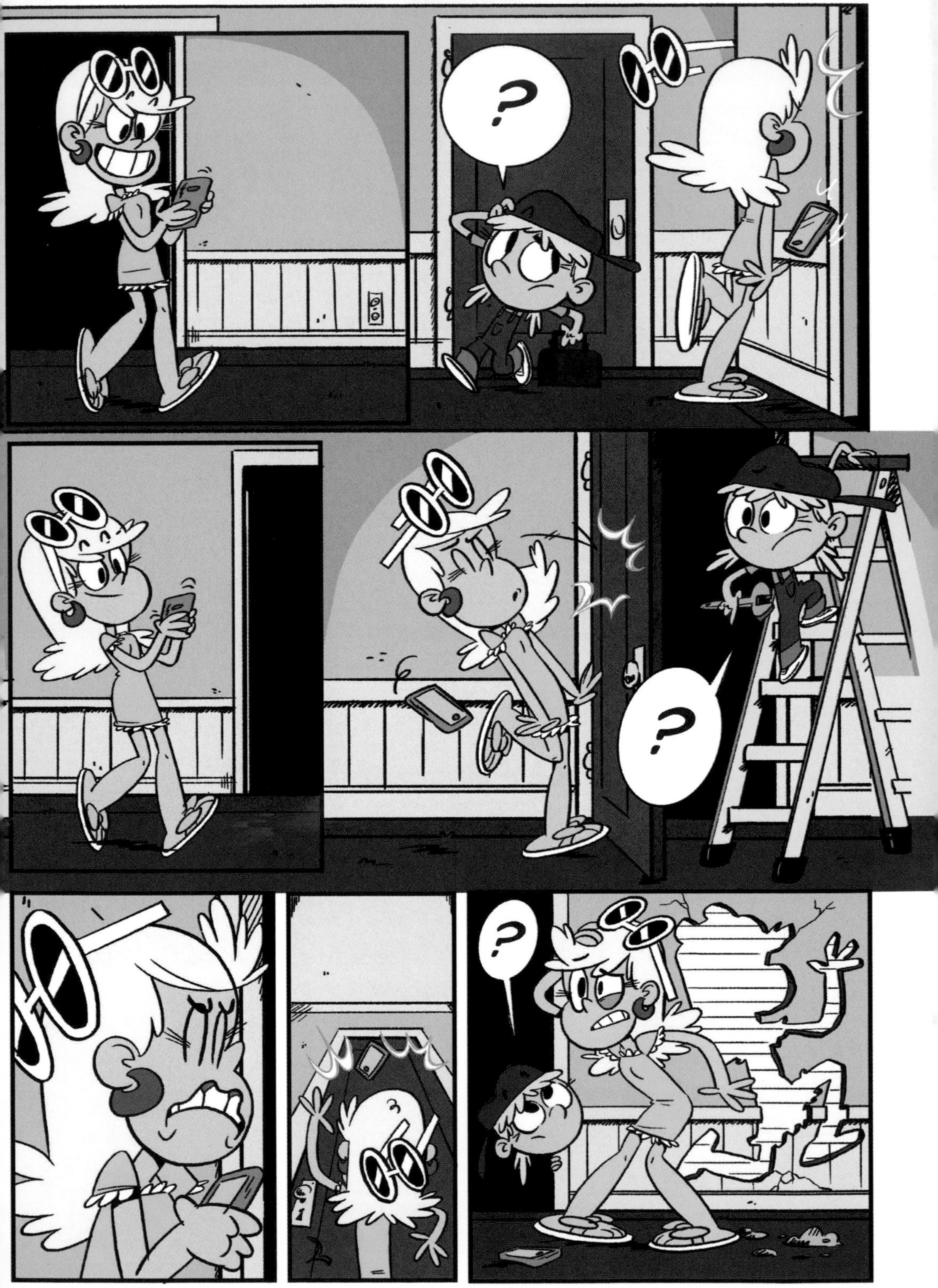
?
?
?

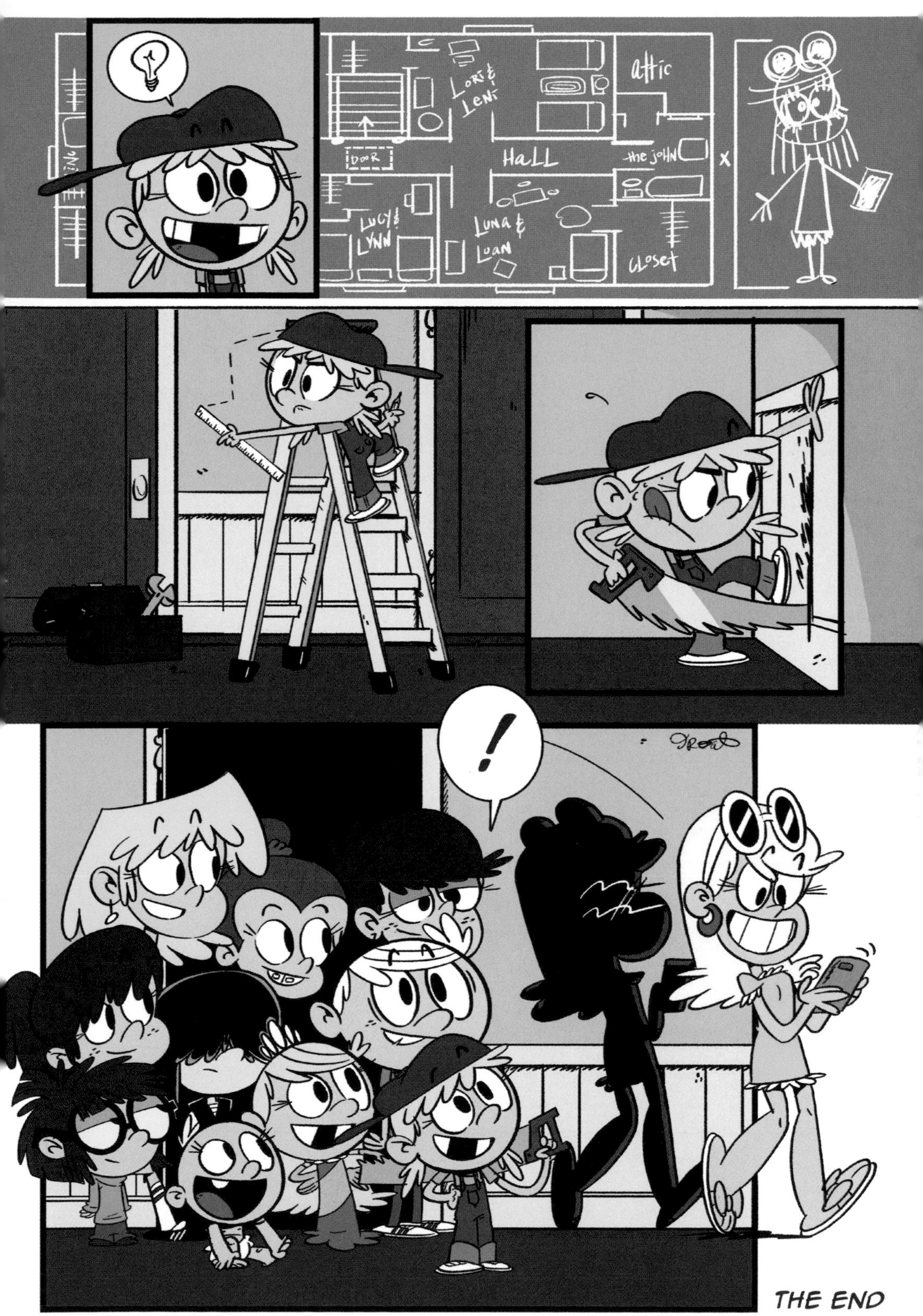
LORI & LENI
attic
DOOR
HALL
the JOHN
LUCY & LYNN
LUNA & LUAN
CLOSET
!

THE END

SPECIAL BONUS FEATURE – AN INTERVIEW WITH...

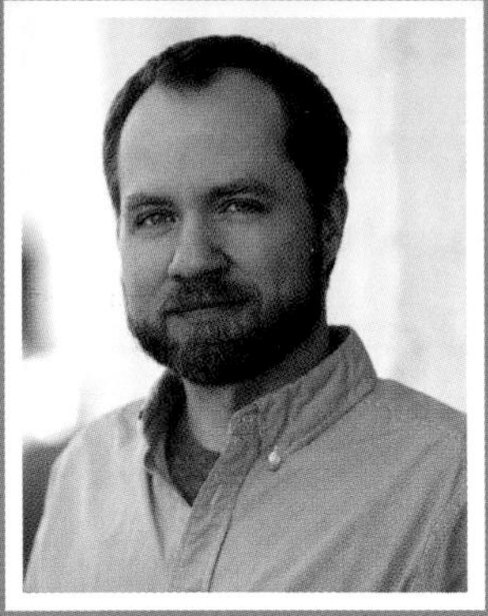

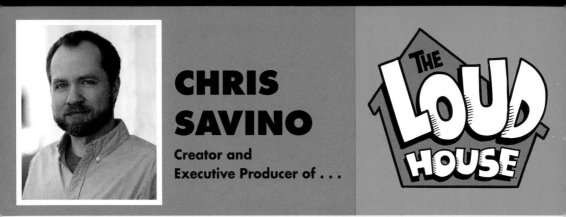

CHRIS SAVINO

Creator and Executive Producer of . . .

THE LOUD HOUSE

Papercutz: *How closely are the episodes based on your real life? Did you have 10 sisters, and where did you grow up?*

Chris Savino: I am from a family with 10 kids, five boys and five girls. My sister's names all begin with "L" and each have only four letters—Lori, Lisa, Lynn, Luan, and Lana. I took those and used them for five of Lincoln's sisters. Lincoln's name comes from the street I grew up on, Lincoln Ave. in Royal Oak, Michigan – a suburb of Detroit. Little snippets of my life experiences make their way into stories, and I encourage everyone on staff to share memories as well.

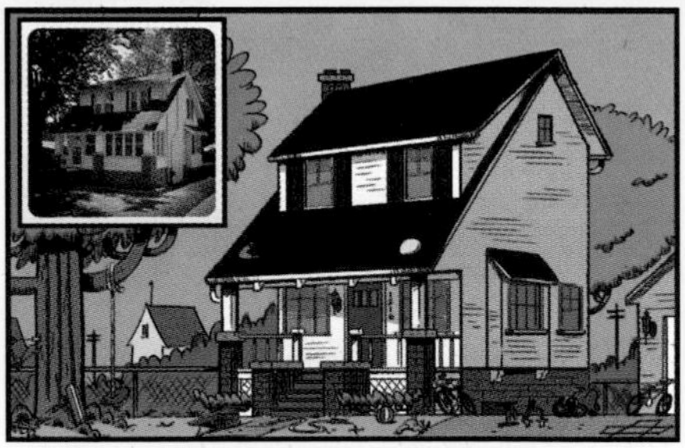

Chris Savino's childhood home inspired the Loud Family home.

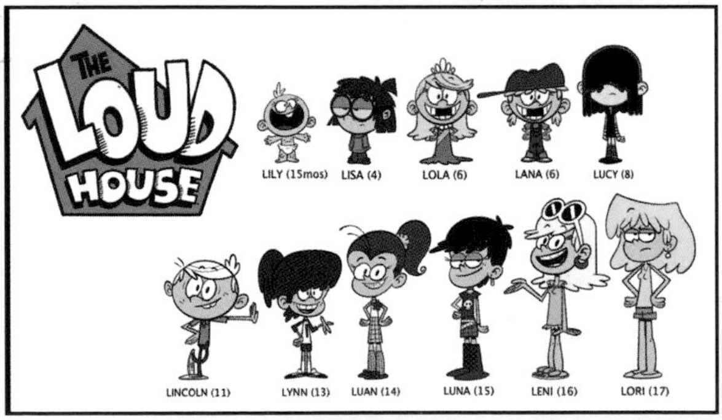
THE LOUD HOUSE
LILY (15mos)
LISA (4)
LOLA (6)
LANA (6)
LUCY (8)
LINCOLN (11)
LYNN (13)
LUAN (14)
LUNA (15)
LENI (16)
LORI (17)

Production designs for the Loud Family.

Papercutz: *Were you influenced on THE LOUD HOUSE by anything in particular?*

Chris Savino: The look of THE LOUD HOUSE is inspired by the Sunday comics I read as a kid: *Peanuts, Dennis the Menace, Garfield, Calvin and Hobbes*...There was something special about opening up the funnies and knowing that the characters you love would be there week after week inviting you into their world. That was what I wanted to achieve for THE LOUD HOUSE. A warm, familiar, and inviting environment (much like my house growing up) where you could be invited in and immediately accepted into the world where you want to hang out and get to know all of the characters.

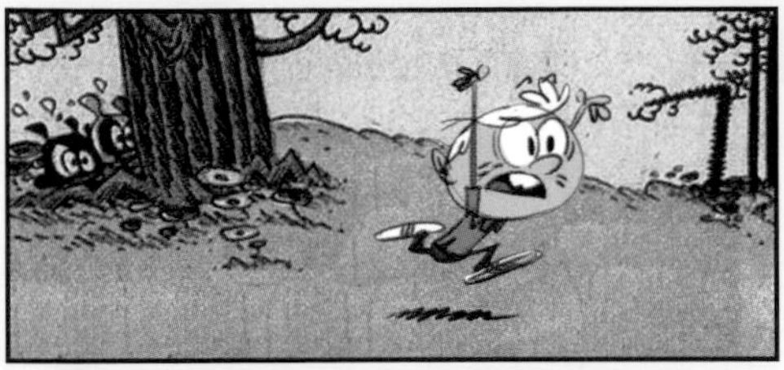

Development sketches of Lincoln Loud.

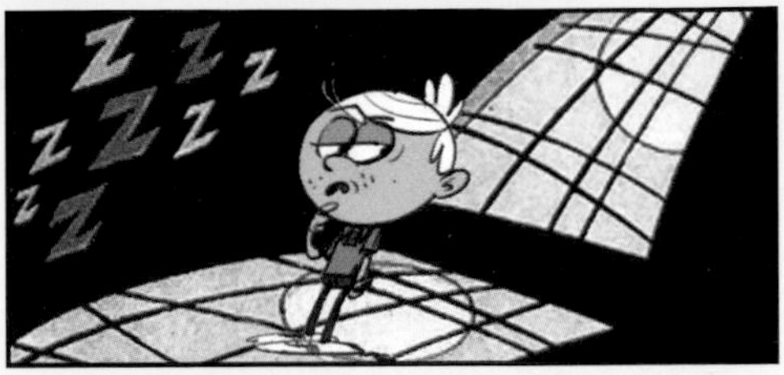

Development sketches of Lincoln Loud.

Papercutz: *Was THE LOUD HOUSE originally envisioned as a family of rabbits? If so, why did you change this?*
Chris Savino: I thought telling the story of a boy rabbit with 25 sisters would be fun, cartoony, and chaotic. I really wanted to do funny animals, but the more I thought about it, the more I realized a human family was the right way to go. Making them human not only made the characters more relatable, but I immediately started pulling from my own life's experiences.

Papercutz: *What have you got up your sleeves for Season 2?*
Chris Savino: In Season 2, we're going to expand Lincoln's experiences and relationships outside of his home and will go more into school. The series will also take a deeper dive into the unique personalities of Lincoln's sisters.

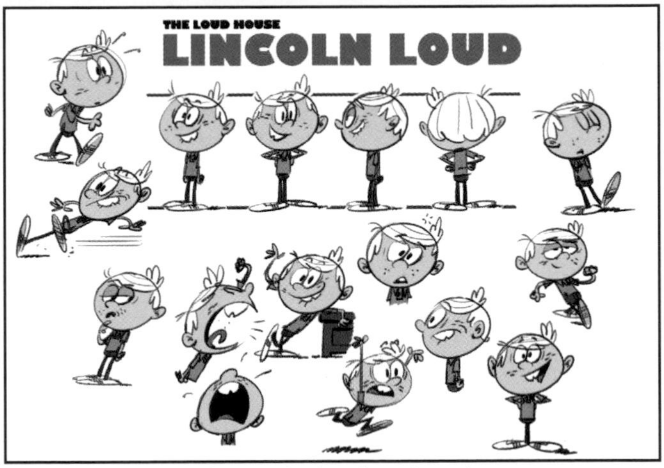
THE LOUD HOUSE
LINCOLN LOUD

Development sketches of Lincoln Loud.

At one point Lincoln was planned to be a rabbit.

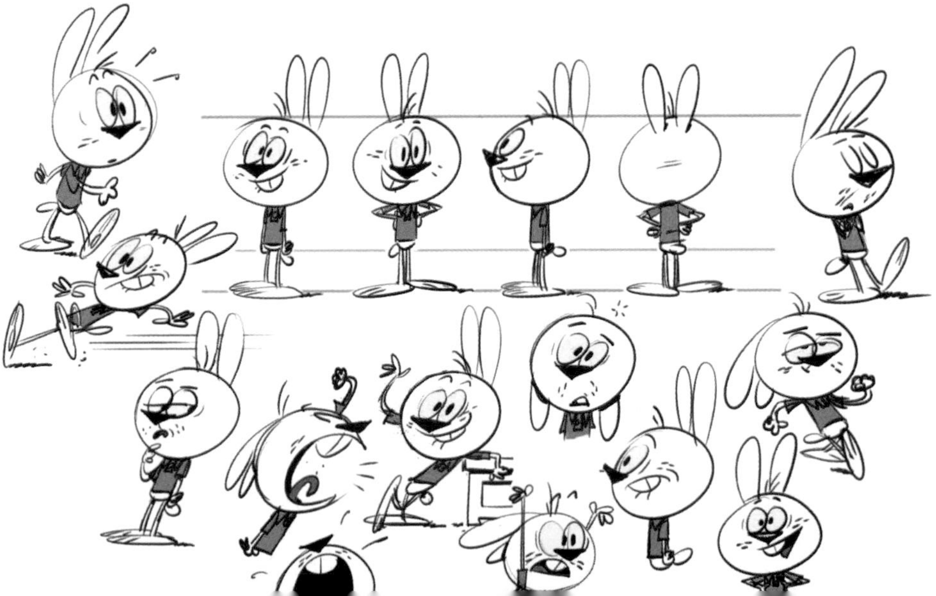

WATCH OUT FOR PAPERCUTZ™

Welcome to the first, family-filled THE LOUD HOUSE graphic novel from Papercutz– those quiet souls dedicated to publishing great graphic novels for all ages. I'm Jim Salicrup, the Editor-in-Chief and a sisterless sibling (I have just one younger brother – Hi, Bill!) and I'm here to talk about the all-new graphic novel series known as THE LOUD HOUSE…

But first, a quick look at the comics history of THE LOUD HOUSE, just to see how we got to this exciting point! Obviously, it all started with the creation, by Chris Savino, of The Loud House animated series on Nickelodeon—for more on that, check out the interview with Chris on page 56. Meanwhile, Papercutz has been publishing graphic novels on the newest and best Nickelodeon animated series, such as SANJAY AND CRAIG, HARVEY BEAKS, and PIG GOAT BANANA CRICKET, so it was just a matter of time before we got to THE LOUD HOUSE. The very first THE LOUD HOUSE comicbook, a minicomic by Chris Savino and Jordan Rosato, was released at the 2015 San Diego Comic-Con. Then, at the 2016 San Diego Comic-Con, a second minicomic was released announcing the official THE LOUD HOUSE graphic novel series.

But something this exciting, this important (especially to loyal fans of THE LOUD HOUSE) just couldn't wait! So, the two mini-comics appeared in NICKELODEON PANDEMONIUM #1 and NICKELODEON PANDEMONIUM #2, reaching fans everywhere. And here's what it's all led up to… the debut of THE LOUD HOUSE #1 "There Will Be Chaos"!

Chris Savino loves comics so much, that he makes it his business to be totally involved in the creation of these terrific graphic novels. I guess coming from a large family helped Chris develop the skills needed to keep track of many things at once. In fact, all the writers and artists who worked on this graphic novel are the same writers and animators who work alongside Chris to create The Loud House cartoons that you see on Nickelodeon! How cool is that?

If this is beginning to sound like a gushing fan letter to Chris Savino and his whole *The Loud House* crew, so be it. We just wanted to let Mr. Savino know how much we appreciate working with him, and everyone else at Nickelodeon, to make these Loud family adventures the best they can possibly be. Let us know what you think by contacting us at the addresses listed below, and stay tuned for the next book: THE LOUD HOUSE #2 "There Will Be *More* Chaos."

And don't forget about the NICKELODEON PANDEMONIUM graphic novels from Papercutz either! Check out the preview on the following pages of the PIG GOAT BANANA CRICKET story from NICKELODEON PANDEMONIUM #2…

Thanks,

Jim

THE HERO

STAY IN TOUCH!

EMAIL: salicrup@papercutz.com
WEB: papercutz.com
TWITTER: @papercutzgn
INSTAGRAM: @papercutzgn
FACEBOOK: PAPERCUTZGRAPHICNOVELS
FANMAIL: Papercutz, 160 Broadway, Suite 700, East Wing, New York, NY 10038

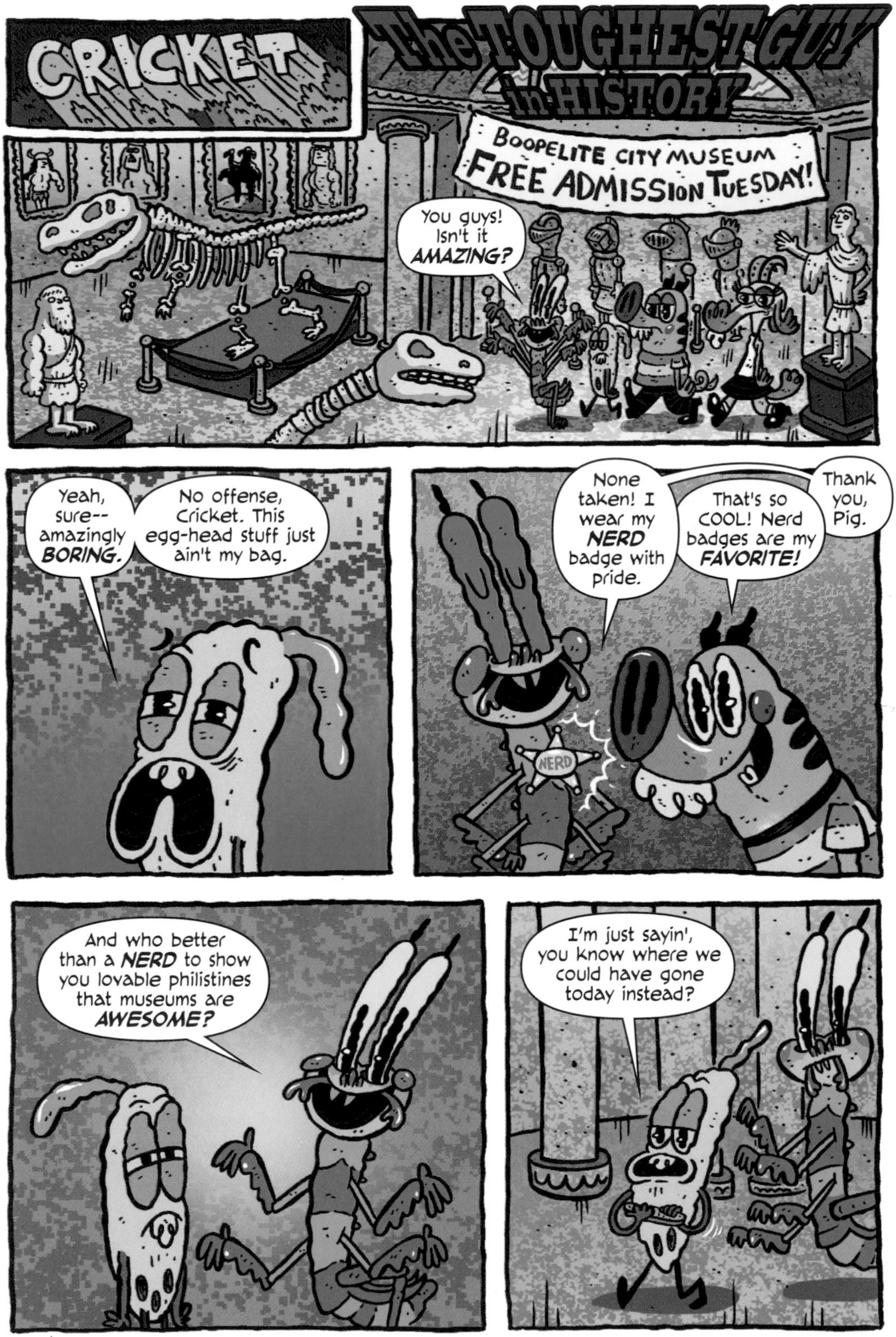
CRICKET
The TOUGHEST GUY in HISTORY
BOOPELITE CITY MUSEUM FREE ADMISSION TUESDAY!
You guys! Isn't it AMAZING?
Yeah, sure-- amazingly BORING.
No offense, Cricket. This egg-head stuff just ain't my bag.
None taken! I wear my NERD badge with pride.
That's so COOL! Nerd badges are my FAVORITE!
Thank you, Pig.
NERD
And who better than a NERD to show you lovable philistines that museums are AWESOME?
I'm just sayin', you know where we could have gone today instead?

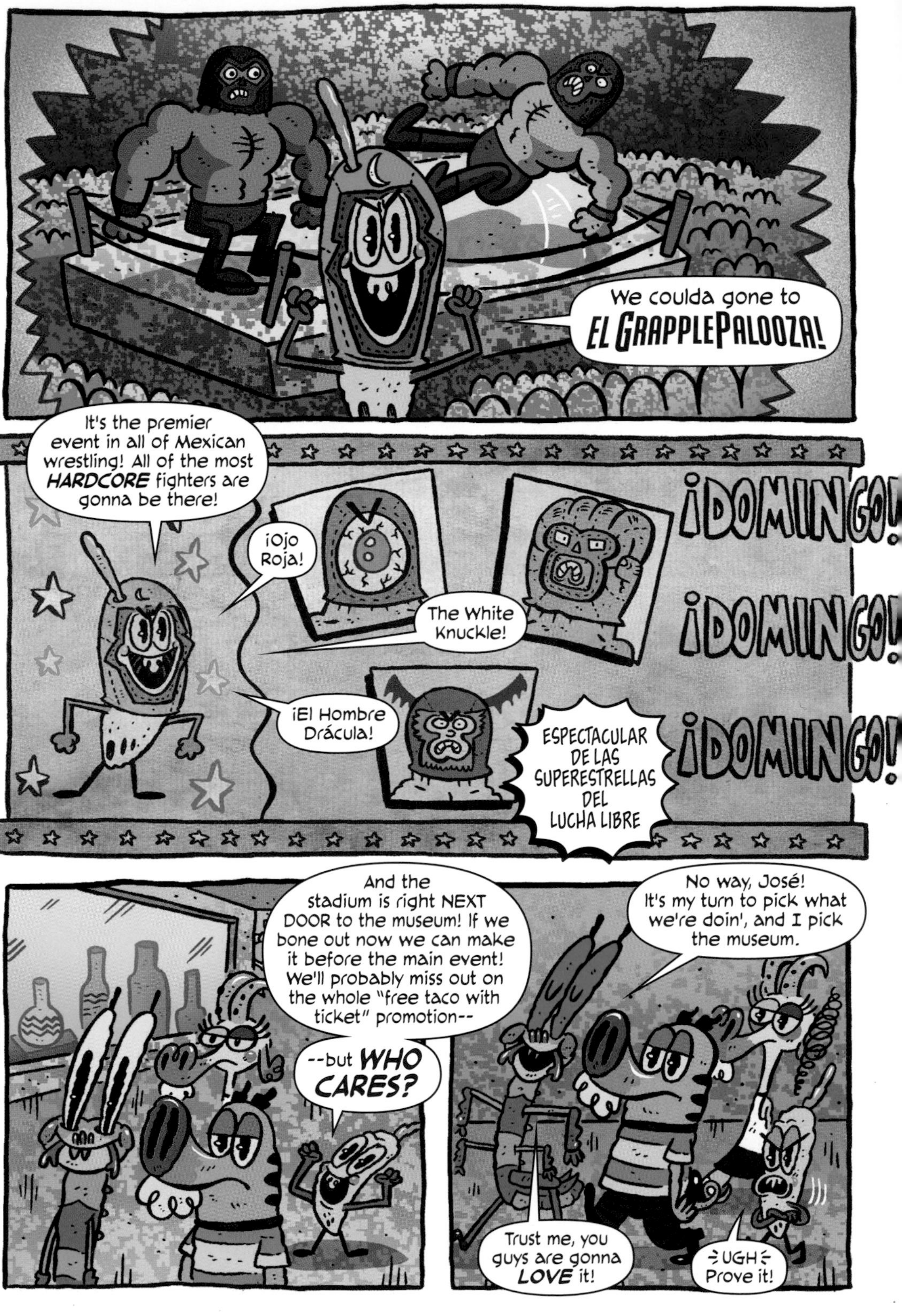
We coulda gone to EL GRAPPLEPALOOZA!
It's the premier event in all of Mexican wrestling! All of the most HARDCORE fighters are gonna be there!
¡Ojo Roja!
The White Knuckle!
¡El Hombre Drácula!
ESPECTACULAR DE LAS SUPERESTRELLAS DEL LUCHA LIBRE
¡DOMINGO! ¡DOMINGO! ¡DOMINGO!
And the stadium is right NEXT DOOR to the museum! If we bone out now we can make it before the main event! We'll probably miss out on the whole "free taco with ticket" promotion--
--but WHO CARES?
No way, José! It's my turn to pick what we're doin', and I pick the museum.
Trust me, you guys are gonna LOVE it!
UGH Prove it!

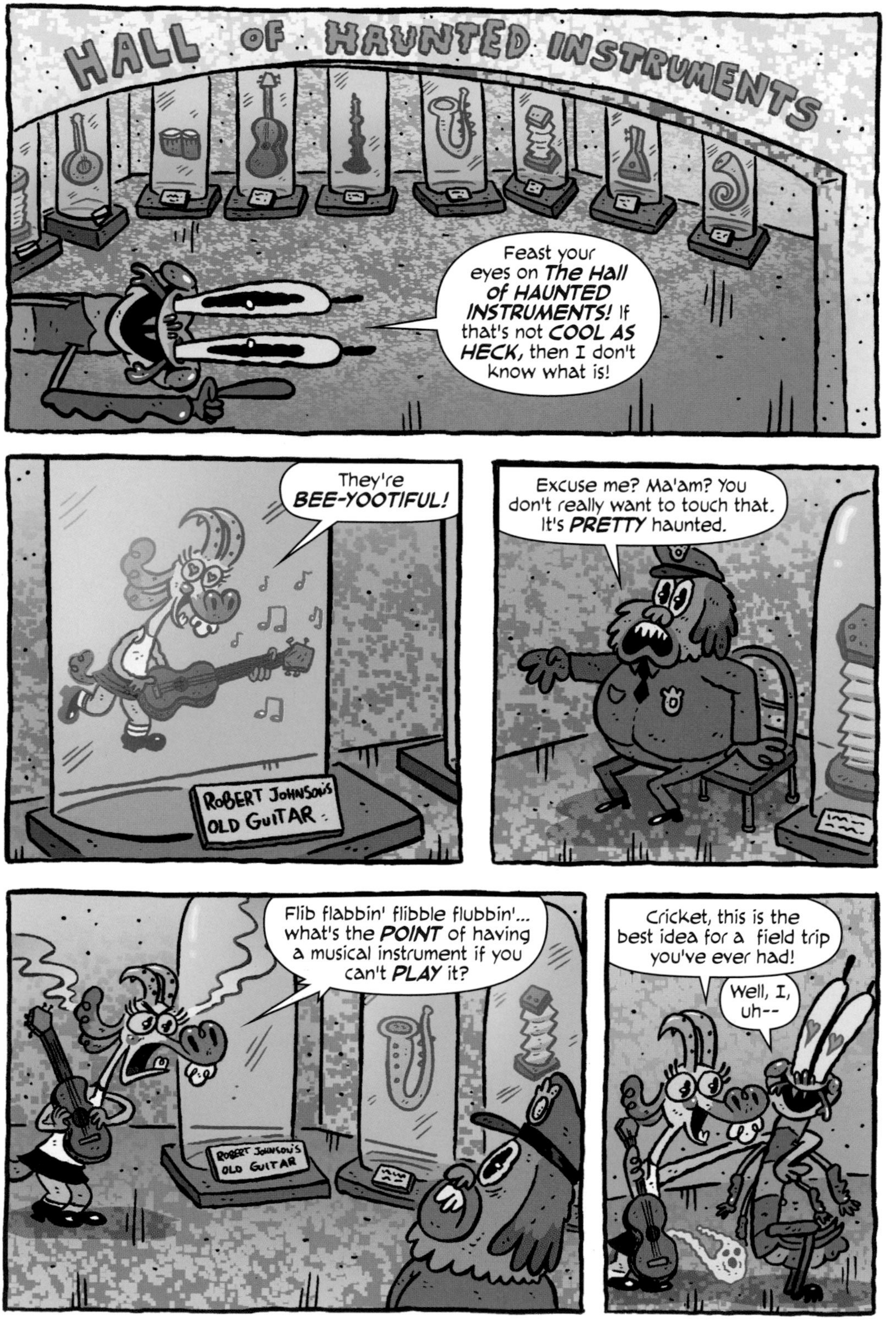
HALL OF HAUNTED INSTRUMENTS
Feast your eyes on The Hall of HAUNTED INSTRUMENTS! If that's not COOL AS HECK, then I don't know what is!
They're BEE-YOOTIFUL!
ROBERT JOHNSON'S OLD GUITAR
Excuse me? Ma'am? You don't really want to touch that. It's PRETTY haunted.
Flib flabbin' flibble flubbin'... what's the POINT of having a musical instrument if you can't PLAY it?
ROBERT JOHNSON'S OLD GUITAR
Cricket, this is the best idea for a field trip you've ever had!
Well, I, uh--

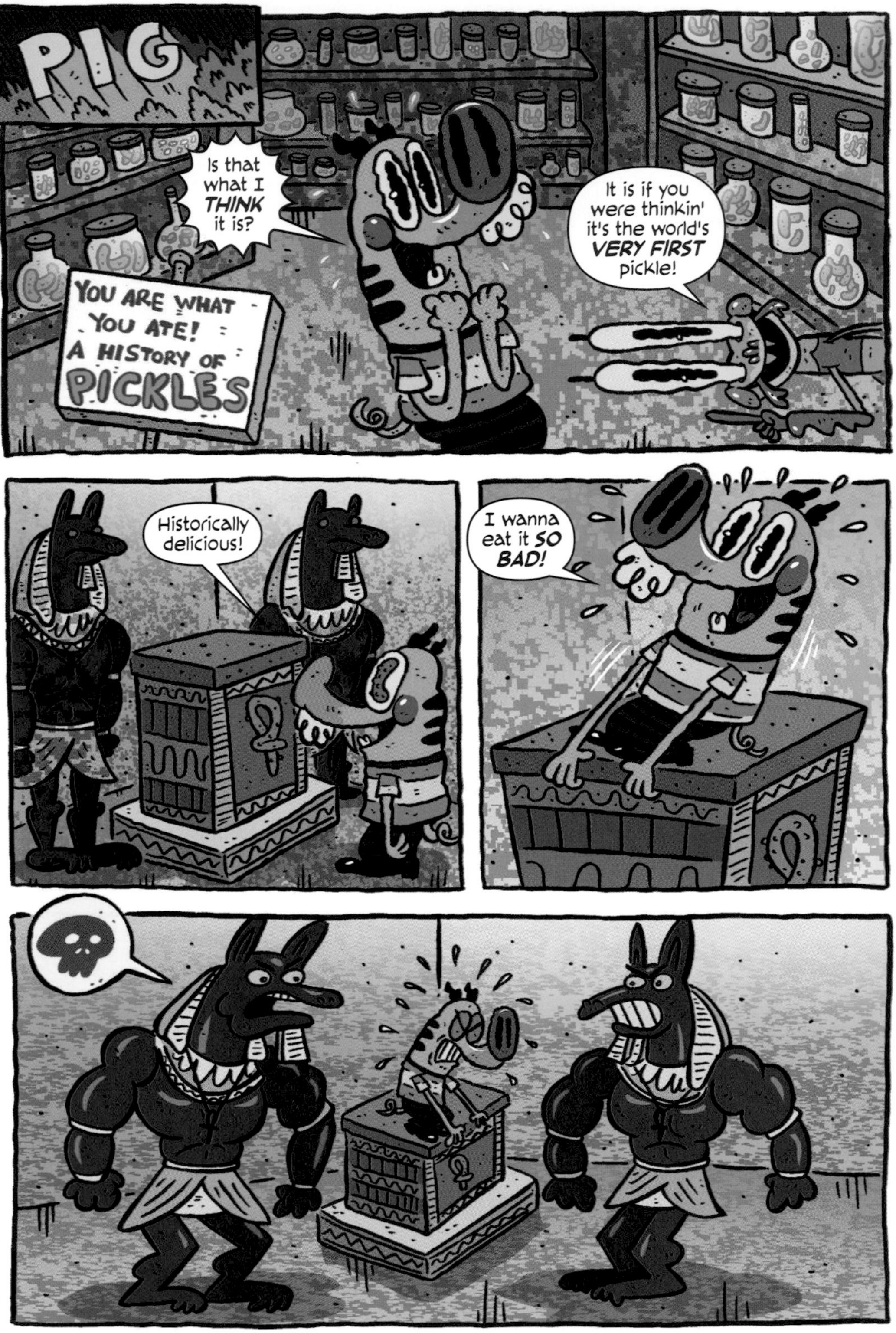
PIG
Is that what I THINK it is?
YOU ARE WHAT YOU ATE! A HISTORY OF PICKLES
It is if you were thinkin' it's the world's VERY FIRST pickle!
Historically delicious!
I wanna eat it SO BAD!

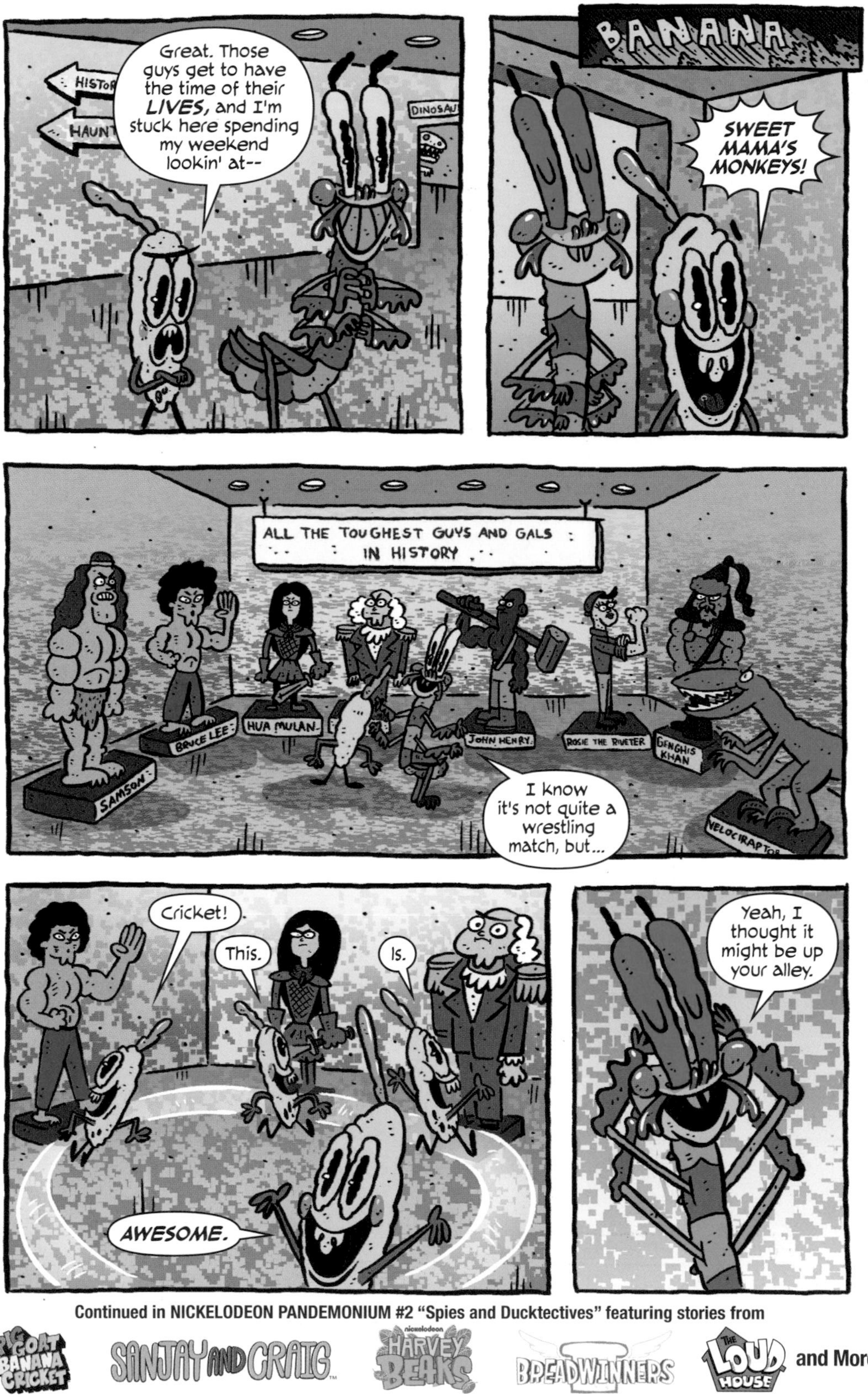

Great. Those guys get to have the time of their *LIVES*, and I'm stuck here spending my weekend lookin' at--
BANANA
SWEET MAMA'S MONKEYS!
ALL THE TOUGHEST GUYS AND GALS IN HISTORY
SAMSON
BRUCE LEE
HUA MULAN
JOHN HENRY
ROSIE THE RIVETER
GENGHIS KHAN
I know it's not quite a wrestling match, but...
Cricket!
This.
Is.
AWESOME.
Yeah, I thought it might be up your alley.

Continued in NICKELODEON PANDEMONIUM #2 "Spies and Ducktectives" featuring stories from

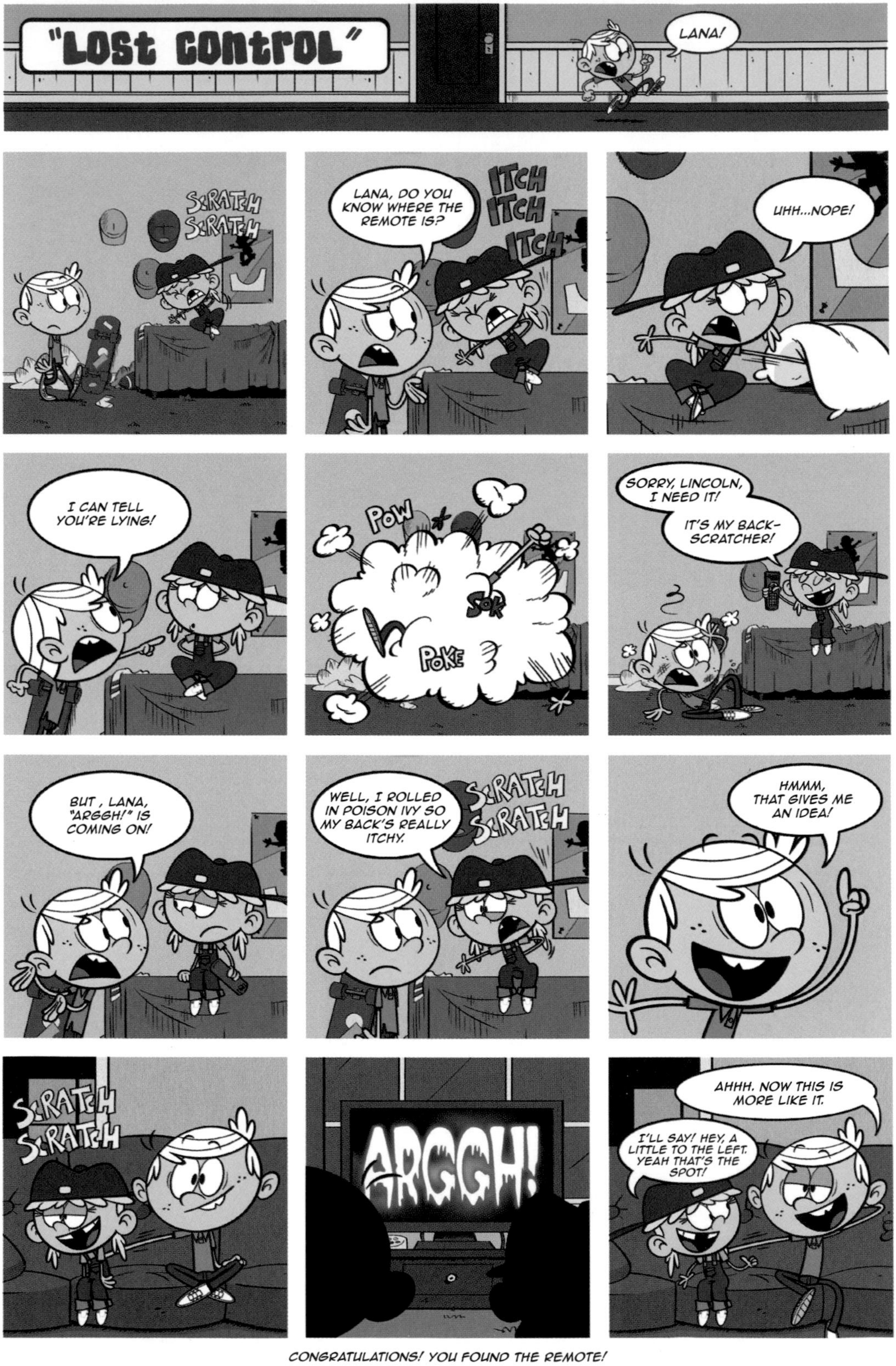
"LOST CONTROL"
LANA!
SCRATCH SCRATCH
LANA, DO YOU KNOW WHERE THE REMOTE IS?
ITCH ITCH ITCH
UHH...NOPE!
I CAN TELL YOU'RE LYING!
POW
SOK
POKE
SORRY, LINCOLN, I NEED IT!
IT'S MY BACK-SCRATCHER!
BUT, LANA, "ARGGH!" IS COMING ON!
WELL, I ROLLED IN POISON IVY SO MY BACK'S REALLY ITCHY.
SCRATCH SCRATCH
HMMM, THAT GIVES ME AN IDEA!
SCRATCH SCRATCH
ARGGH!
AHHH. NOW THIS IS MORE LIKE IT.
I'LL SAY! HEY, A LITTLE TO THE LEFT. YEAH THAT'S THE SPOT!

CONGRATULATIONS! YOU FOUND THE REMOTE!